DEATH ON HANOVER

A HIGGINS & HAWKE MYSTERY

LEE STRAUSS

Death on Hanover

© 2019 Lee Strauss

La Plume Press

3205-415 Commonwealth Road

Kelowna, BC, Canada

V4V 2M4

www.laplumepress.com

ISBN: 978-1-77409-061-9

1

_____

Sam Hawke, an investigative reporter for *The Boston Daily Record*, consoled herself. You couldn't break a big story every day. Her deal with her editor, Archie August, was that she'd continue to lead the ladies' pages as per her original agreement when he'd allowed her to move from receptionist to reporter, even though she was a married woman. Jobs were scarce and men resented sharing them with women who were supposedly supported by their husbands.

Supposedly, Samantha thought as she snapped photographs of the fundraiser held at St. Stephen's Church on Hanover Street. Her louse of a husband, Seth Rosenbaum, had skipped town years ago and left her with their young daughter and his ornery mother. Well, enough was enough. She couldn't be expected to wait for him forever, and the good Lord knew, with the kind of reckless life he led and the nefarious company he kept, he could good and well be dead.

"Miss Hawke?" Hawke was her maiden name, and the byline Sam Hawke had a *non-female* ring to it. At least with the printed press, her blond locks and curvy form couldn't be discriminated against.

Mr. Mulryan, the church secretary, wore cuffed pants, a well-worn cardigan over a shirt and tie, and scuffed-on-the-toes leather loafers. With hair and nails neatly trimmed, and smoothly shaven skin on his long face, he had an effeminate quality. To raise money for widows and orphans, he'd organized the clothing bazaar.

Samantha responded, "Yes, Mr. Mulryan."

"Thank you for agreeing to cover our affair. Since the panic, there are so many more people in need, and we at St. Stephen's church are here to help out any way we can."

Putting aside her camera, Samantha removed a notebook and pencil from her leather messenger bag. "If someone needs clothing or another kind of help, who should they contact?" she asked.

"I'm the person they can come to first." Mr. Mulryan gave Samantha a telephone number. "Of course, Father O'Hara is always here on Sundays, and we do hope to see more people attend mass this weekend."

St. Stephen's church attracted the Irish, but everyone felt the pinch of the Depression, no matter their ethnicity.

"I'm sure your efforts are appreciated," Samantha said.

The door flew open, and a middle-aged woman screeched, "There's a dead man in the churchyard!"

Samantha looked at Mr. Mulryan. Dead people in a churchyard wasn't so unusual, except for the fact that there wasn't a cemetery attached to St. Stephen's sanctuary.

Mr. Mulryan stepped toward the distraught woman. "Are you certain, Mrs. Breen?"

Mrs. Breen seemed to get her nerves under control. "I've buried two husbands and a father, Mr. Mulryan. I know a dead body when I see it."

Samantha followed the odd pair out the front door and around the corner on the Clark Street side of the building. The body of a man lay along the short fence.

"It's partially hidden by that shrub," Mrs. Breen said, gloved hand to her heart. "And if a bee hadn't landed on my shoulder, I wouldn't have jumped and turned my head. At first, I only glimpsed a shoe and thought it was a vagrant sleeping it off."

Samantha reached the man on the lawn just as the lady completed her long-winded explanation.

Mrs. Breen wasn't wrong. Whoever this poor soul was—twisted unnaturally onto his side—he was clearly not breathing. No one would be with that gash across his neck. Samantha was a little ashamed at her next thought: *Finally*! A story of her own.

She turned to Mr. Mulryan. "I'll stay with the body while you call the police."

SAMANTHA WAS PLEASED that the bile that rose in the back of her throat subsided quickly—faster than in the past when she'd been exposed to a dead body—especially where blood was involved. Intrinsically, she knew she had precious little time before the hordes of police and journalists descended, and took the opportunity to snap as many pictures as possible. She carefully set the exposure. The light was getting low. Would she need a greater aperture?

Mrs. Breen inexplicably remained, a handkerchief pressed to her face.

"I'm fine to watch over the body until Mr. Mulryan returns and the police arrive," Samantha said.

Mrs. Breen didn't take the hint. "I find the whole concept of death fascinating," she said, her handkerchief out like a flag. "One second you're alive and bam!

The next, you're talking to Saint Peter at the pearly gates."

The woman must be in shock, Samantha thought. As soon as she was done getting the story, Samantha decided she'd find out where Mrs. Breen lived and take her home. Meanwhile, a few questions wouldn't hurt.

"Do you recognize this man?"

Mrs. Breen shook her head. "He looks to be Italian. I'm Irish," she said as if the two ethnicities never had reason to meet or socialize.

Samantha wasn't a doctor, though now that she and Dr. Haley Higgins, Boston's assistant chief medical examiner, had become friends, she was a little more familiar with the basics—like how rigor mortis worked. With a tentative touch, she could tell the victim's limbs were stiff, which meant the syndrome had set in and the man had died over four hours ago. Who knew how much longer he would've gone unnoticed if it hadn't been for Mrs. Breen's bee? Samantha sniffed and wrinkled her nose. With this streak of warm weather, someone would've smelled him soon enough.

Mr. Mulryan returned, puffing from his jog to his office telephone and back.

"The police are on their way."

Recognizing her window for snapping photos had closed, Samantha put the lens cap on the camera. She carefully stowed it in its leather case and tightened down the strap to keep the expensive piece of equipment from sliding out.

"What's going on, Mr. Mulryan?" A shrill female voice reached them from the other side of the hedge. Mr. Mulryan went into action, turning his back to the dead man as a shield.

"It's nothing, Mrs. Jones. Go on inside. Lovely things available to purchase and such a good cause."

Mr. Mulryan's gaze rested on Mrs. Breen. "Shall we find Mr. Breen?"

"I suppose." The lady sniffed. "There's not much I can do for this poor fellow."

A bug-eyed Ford police cruiser screeched to a stop. A uniformed policeman and a pinched-faced detective in civilian clothes stepped out of the boxy machine and slammed the doors. Mr. Mulryan approached and said a few words Samantha couldn't hear before he took Mrs. Breen inside.

Samantha recognized both men and smiled at the sight of the younger one, Officer Tom Bell. She and Tom had become acquainted through a mishap at an illegal speakeasy. He'd been on an undercover mission, and she was hot on a story. When she'd saved his life, he'd become her police contact. He would've been interested in more than friendship if she hadn't put a stop to it. Tom was an agreeable man with attractive features. A fellow who lived by the book, which Samantha admired, but it wasn't a philosophy she could always abide by in her profession. Plus, there was Seth. There was always Seth.

"Hello, Tom," she said.

His eyes widened in surprise. "Samantha. What are you doing here already?"

Tom would've expected her to show up with the flock of journalists sure to be screeching to the curb any minute. Samantha wasn't the only one with a police contact.

"I was working on a story for the ladies' pages. The summer bazaar here is quite popular and of interest to the community."

Detective Cluney was at Officer Bell's elbow. Beefy in stature and gruff in nature, the detective wasn't one for pleasantries. Another cruiser pulled up behind the first one, and an officer with a camera approached with long, relaxed strides. After a quick greeting, he took photographs in the same manner Samantha had earlier. She made sure to keep her camera strapped over her shoulder and pushed toward her back. The detective would frown at her presumption and accuse her of interfering if it looked like it had been in use.

Detective Cluney nodded at Samantha in

acknowledgment. "Miss Hawke, how did you first learn of the body in the yard?"

"Mrs. Breen, a parishioner at St. Stephen's, noticed it then announced her discovery after she entered the church in distress."

Just as Samantha had predicted, members of the press began driving up, and Samantha saw Johnny Milwaukee's tall form in the midst. His felt fedora sat crookedly on his head, and his persistent wry grin was plastered to his face. Samantha smirked, staying out of her colleague's line of sight. They weren't enemies, but Samantha didn't consider him a chum either. Fierce competitors were what they were, and she'd take whatever advantage she could gain.

"Who's the dead guy?" Johnny shouted out to no avail. Detective Cluney didn't pander to the press, and none of the other officers would dare to answer without their boss's go-ahead.

Dr. Haley Higgins, assistant to the chief medical examiner, was the next to arrive and stepped around the throng. A tall, no-nonsense woman, Haley Higgins was intelligent, insightful, and driven. Wild curls refused to be tamed into place, and the doctor often forwent the style of the day for a practical ponytail under a simple hat. Haley arched her dark brow at Samantha when she spotted her.

8

"I was already here," Samantha explained preemptively. "Covering the fundraiser."

"Hello, Detective and Officers," Haley said. She stopped short before the body and stared.

Hesitation at the sight of a body was so unlike the pathologist, Samantha felt a note of concern. "Dr. Higgins? Is everything all right?"

HALEY SNAPPED her gaping mouth shut. She'd seen plenty of stabbing deaths in her line of work, and neck lacerations weren't uncommon. That wasn't what bothered her.

"Who found the body?"

"A parishioner," Samantha said, "on her way to the bazaar."

Haley scanned the small crowd of investigators. "Did anyone move the body?"

Detective Cluney puffed on a newly lit cigar. "What's on your mind, Dr. Higgins?"

Haley didn't want to mention the real reason her pulse jumped, and she didn't have to. Other evidence was present. "There's no blood pooling on the grass. With the nature of these wounds, it was likely that he bled to death."

"So, he was moved here," Detective Cluney said. "Bell, go find this Mrs. Breen and have her brought in for questioning. Maybe she saw something she doesn't know is significant."

Haley caught Officer Bell's quick glance in Samantha's direction. The poor fellow was in trouble, but matters of the heart weren't Haley's concern. She had her own problems in that regard. Officer Jack Thompson, to be specific, a crime scene photographer and former love. With camera in hand, he awkwardly hovered over her as she squatted beside the corpse.

"Dr. Higgins," he said. "Are you all right?"

Haley forced a smile. Jack had returned to Boston, and she could do nothing about it. Even though she'd made it clear that she wasn't interested, that she was a mistress to her work, he seemed undaunted. Haley was at an age where the word *spinster* was used to describe her and accurately so. Despite all of that, she'd still agreed to attend the policeman's ball on his arm. *It was a good cause.* She'd told herself that was why she'd said yes.

Haley asked a question back. "Do you find the positioning of the body unusual?"

"For a body dump? No."

Haley nodded and returned to her examination. Blood and bruising on the corpse's face. A laceration on his neck. Pulling the man's fists clear of his body, Haley noted contusions on the tops of his knuckles. "He's been in a fight."

"Nothing new for hooligans," Detective Cluney said as he lit a cigar. "Our man here got in bad company, and it got out of hand. Was dumped at the church out of guilt, I'm bettin'. Wanted the guy to be found."

"Any clue to where the crime might've taken place?" This was from Samantha who, for the moment, had been forgotten by Detective Cluney.

"Why are you still here?" he barked.

Samantha put her shoulders back and looked the detective straight in the eye. "I was one of the first on the scene."

"Then you'll be called to the station to give a statement. I'm not taking questions from reporters right now, Miss Hawke." Detective Cluney blew smoke out of the side of his mouth as he stared Samantha down. She shrugged at Haley. "See you later, Doctor."

"You're still coming for dinner tomorrow?" Haley asked.

Samantha smiled. "Wouldn't miss it."

"Do you have an answer?" Detective Cluney asked with impatience, once Samantha was gone.

"About?"

"Clues for the scene of the crime. Where the fight happened?"

Haley checked the dead man's pockets. Empty.

"Nothing definitive at the moment," Haley said.

She stood and brushed dry grass off her skirt. "The postmortem might tell us more."

The ambulance had arrived, and the detective released the body. The members of the press asked their questions, but when Haley searched for Samantha among them, her friend was nowhere to be found.

2

Once inside the *Boston Daily Record*, Samantha removed her hat and gloves and put them in her desk drawer. The "pit", as they called the newsroom, was on the second floor of a tall, narrow building on Water Street. A collection of desks, each piled high with newspapers, was littered with short pencils, and accessorized with dirty ashtrays, overused coffee mugs, and upright black typewriters. Samantha smirked at the sight of Johnny's empty desk and the absence of shy Max Owen, Johnny's puppy dog photographer. Freddy Hall, the beefy sports reporter, sneered in her direction. He wasn't one to keep his views about women working and "taking a man's job" to himself, and Samantha had learned to give him a wide berth. No sense poking the bees' nest.

Samantha grabbed her camera and ducked in at the

editor's office. For a change, she had the scoop! Archie August was the atypical patriarch of the news team. A set of round spectacles was pushed up on his short nose in the middle of his round face. The sleeves of a wrinkled cotton shirt were rolled up to the crook of his puffy elbows, and leather suspenders dug into thick shoulders. The room was full of blue smoke from the cigar that burned in the ashtray.

"Miss Hawke," Mr. August growled. "I'm a busy man."

"I think I have a story."

"Don't make me guess it."

"A body was found at St. Stephen's Church."

Mr. August picked up his cigar and puffed. "Weren't you doing a fluff piece there?"

"Yes, which was why I was the first on the scene, even before the police."

The editor stared back with bulbous eyes; his interest garnered. "Go on."

"I got the statement from the witness who found the body and comments from the police." Samantha didn't mention those were off the record. She tapped her camera. "I got pictures, and I want the story."

"Where's Milwaukee?"

Samantha's jaw tightened. No way on God's green earth was she going to let Johnny snag this story from underneath her. "I have no idea. He's not at his desk."

Mr. August flicked his thick fingers in her direction. "Very well. See what you can do. I want it on my desk for tonight's paper, and if there's dirt, I want that too."

Samantha hurried down the hall before Mr. August could change his mind, and took the elevator down one floor to where the darkroom was located, just beyond the composing room. She waved briefly to the manager there, Inky Isaacson, who waved ink-stained fingers in return, but she didn't stop to chat. That would come after she'd had a chance to write up a story. First, she needed to get these photos developed. Then she needed to talk to Haley.

Her hand slipped into her jacket pocket, and her fingers, as if on a mission of their own, fished for the torn strip of paper concealed there. Her heart skipped a beat. Taking it from the body was probably a crime, definitely a misdemeanor, but she'd deal with that problem later.

The darkroom was unoccupied, and after turning on the red light, she hung the DO NOT DISTURB sign on the door. Jars filled with the chemical solutions sat on one shelf, and she filled an empty tray before unrolling her film. After creating the negatives, she watched the magic of science process her images onto white sheets of paper, which never ceased to fascinate Samantha—even if what developed before her eyes was a gruesome crime scene. She fished the sheets out of the trays with a pair of tongs and pinned them to a line to dry. She perused the images for anything that could be evidence of the "dirt" Mr. August was after, but nothing jumped out at her.

Returning to the pit, Samantha saw that Johnny and Max had returned. Johnny jawed as usual with sour-faced Freddy Hall, who reported on sports, specifically baseball this time of year. Samantha strolled to her chair and threaded a piece of crisp white paper into the roller of her black typewriter.

Johnny, who Samantha knew cast glances her way when he thought she couldn't see him, finally gave her his full attention.

"Hey doll, you missed all the action."

She fluttered her thick eyelashes innocently. "What do you mean?"

"The body at the church." Johnny pulled on a cigarette, releasing the smoke through his nose. "I'm afraid you left the fundraiser before the real story happened."

Samantha flashed a cocky smile. "I'm not sure who your source is, Johnny, but I'd get a new one."

Johnny leaned forward with raised brows. "Are you saying you were there?"

"I don't have to say anything to you, except this is my story. You can ask the boss yourself."

Johnny laughed and slapped the top of his desk. "Hot damn! Look at you, intrepid lady reporter."

"Don't make fun of me, Johnny! I won't have it."

Johnny snuffed out his cigarette and sauntered over to Samantha's desk, his grin crooked, and his hair mussed. She frowned in disapproval as he leaned casually against her desk.

"How about I make you a deal, doll?" he said. "You tell me what you got, and I'll tell you what I got."

He leaned so close that Samantha could smell his aftershave. She placed a palm on his arm and pushed him away. "No deal."

"Huh." Johnny wrinkled his nose and worked his lips. "You must really have somethin' then. Normally, you jump at getting what you can from me."

The way he said that suggested an innuendo Samantha didn't appreciate. "Stop bothering me. I've got work to do."

Johnny stepped back toward his desk. "Right. The fundraiser piece." He glanced at the door and back to Samantha, then raised a brow. "Where were you, anyways, Miss Hawke?"

"Not that it's your business, but I was at the ladies —" The moment the words escaped her mouth, she knew she'd made a mistake. She had been too quick to give an explanation. Johnny pivoted for the door. "You were in the darkroom, weren't ya?"

"Johnny!"

Johnny broke into a trot, and Samantha raced after him. Darned heels! Johnny kept at least two paces ahead and skipped down the stairs. Samantha could take the elevator, but it was notoriously slow. She held the railing and ran down the steps.

"Johnny!"

The men in the composing area stopped at the commotion Samantha and Johnny had created, and try as Samantha might, she couldn't get in front of Johnny to prevent him from entering the darkroom first. He snapped on the red light.

Her prints hung in a neat row on full display.

Johnny whistled as he took them in. "You little minx. How'd you get these?"

Samantha snapped them from the pins before Johnny could get a good look. "I was at the scene when the body was found. I took them before the police arrived."

Johnny stared at Samantha with a look of admiration. "We really ought to get on the same team."

"Not on your life."

Johnny had a reputation for playing "fair" only when it suited him. His scruples were in question, and Samantha had more than her own welfare to think of. Talia came first. Her daughter was the reason for everything Samantha did, including this job.

She was struck with a shard of guilt. Here she was condemning Johnny for his scruples when, only a couple of hours ago, she had removed evidence from a corpse.

The question now was, what should she do about it?

THE JOHN DOE lay on the ceramic table, ready to be washed down.

Dr. Peter Guthrie, a recent English immigrant and new Chief Medical Examiner, approached with interest in his watery eyes. He took great strides with legs so long and thin that the image of a cricket ready to spring came to mind.

"Dead as a doornail?" he asked his lips twitching.

"He didn't die at the church," Haley said. "The body was moved."

"I see." The white bushes above his eyes furrowed into one long hedge. "No identification on his person?"

"None. Not even a wallet."

"A mugging gone wrong?"

"It's possible. Whatever the case, the victim was used to scrapping." Haley displayed the bruising on the body. "Yellow, green, and black mixed. New bruising on old."

She turned over the right wrist. "A double spider tattoo. They appear to be fighting."

"Looks a bit gaunt," Dr. Guthrie added. "A soup-line bloke?"

"Could be. His suit was threadbare, and he doesn't appear to have washed lately, though he did bother to shave this morning. He has a recent cut on his chin."

"Shaking hand? A drinker?"

Prohibition failed to keep alcohol out of the hands of those who wanted it, and backyard distilleries not only made the quality dreadfully low, it was sometimes deadly.

Haley sighed her condolences, then with a sharp scalpel, started the Y incision on the man's chest. A bone cutter opened the ribcage, and after propping the ribs open, she carefully removed each organ one by one, examining and weighing it. Soon a queue of organs, each in a porcelain tray, lined a side table.

The stomach contents confirmed Dr. Guthrie's prediction. Along with a recent meal of bread and canned meat, Haley smelled the bitter scent of cheap whiskey.

She collected blood samples to send to the lab.

Mr. Martin, the primary intern at the morgue, blew through the doors. In his mid-twenties, the medical student was earnest if not timely.

"So sorry I'm late," he said as he whipped off his

hat and cotton suit jacket. "Traffic jam on Cambridge Bridge blocked the passage of my bus. I haven't missed it, have I?"

"You're just in time to sew him up."

"Rats! Anything interesting?"

"Nothing out of the ordinary."

Mr. Martin studied the body. "The guy took a beating."

Haley agreed. "He did."

"Cause of death?" Mr. Martin asked.

"He bled out. Carotid artery severed."

Haley washed up at the large ceramic sink then returned to her desk. The morgue, though in the hospital basement, was a brightly lit room painted white. Two operating tables took up the center of the room with various tables and cupboards lining the walls. From her spot at her desk near the front of the room, she could see both Mr. Martin at work in the surgery to her right and Dr. Guthrie through his office window straight ahead.

She stared at the telephone. Should she call Detective Cluney? She didn't have anything new to report and wouldn't until the laboratory results came in, but she'd like to know if he'd discovered anything new.

Haley picked up the telephone, but instead of putting in a call to the detective, she asked to speak to Officer Thompson.

"Thompson," Jack said when he picked up.

"Hi, Jack, it's Haley."

Jack's voice immediately softened. "Oh, hello."

"I'm sorry to bother you, but I'm wondering if you've developed the photographs from the scene

"Not yet. Why? Did you find anything?"

"No, I just thought maybe you did. I wouldn't mind having a look. Would that be possible?"

"Ah, Haley, you know how Cluney is. Need to know basis. I'd have to give him a reason."

"Of course, forgive me."

"It's okay, just give me a reason."

"I can't yet, but I'll let you know when I have one."

Haley regretted calling Jack Thompson. Trying to call in a favor was impulsive. However, now that she thought about it, she remembered that Samantha had had a camera on her at the scene. Ten to one she'd snapped photographs before the police got there. Haley wanted another look at the positioning of the body. She'd seen a photo of the exact same thing once before: a man twisted on his side, neck slashed.

Her brother, Joe Higgins.

THE POLICEMAN's ball was an event organized by the department to honor policemen of valor, remember those who had lost their lives while on duty, and to raise money for their widows and children who, during these depressive times, needed all the help they could get.

Haley usually supported the effort from behind the scenes, since she wasn't a member of the force or close to anyone on it, so it came as a big surprise when Jack Thompson had asked her to accompany him. She had been reluctant to do so at first, but Jack was rather persistent, and it was a good cause. Besides, it wouldn't hurt her to build up goodwill with members of the Boston police force, since she did step on their toes, so to speak, during her personal inquiries.

At the moment, there was literal stepping on toes going on as she and Jack danced to the live band playing in the hall.

"I'm sorry," Haley said, feeling a blush rise to her cheeks. "I played baseball with my brothers growing up. I'm not much of a dancer."

Jack chuckled. "Thankfully, it's not a competition."

Most women in the room were wives, mothers, or sisters of someone on the force. There were a few female officers, but police work continued to be a man's domain. Happily for Haley, Samantha was also at the ball, on the arm of Officer Tom Bell, whose eyes expressed pure delight as he led his date around the dance floor.

Jack looked dapper in loose-fitting, high-waist black

dress pants, a crisp white high-collared shirt, topped with a fitted suit jacket with glossy black lapels, which had a single button fastened. He dipped his chin with a look of admiration at Haley's lime-green satin gown, which flowed gently from shoulder to floor and was suitable for the festivities. Though she preferred simple dress suits for work, or the more practical slacks —pants for women—that were becoming increasingly popular for ladies, her wardrobe contained a surprising number of fancy dresses because she and her good friend Dr. Gerald Mitchell often attended the theater or the opera or such events together. It was a mutually agreeable and platonic agreement. Gerald was devoted to his wife, who'd been bedridden and mentally incoherent for many years.

Jack, on the other hand, stirred feelings in Haley that she'd rather not have admitted to. He'd broken her heart by leaving town suddenly after Joe had died. Jack was a restless man, and she would not let him have her heart again, just to abandon it on a whim.

They shared a table with Detective Cluney and his wife.

"Are you enjoying yourself, Mrs. Cluney?" Haley asked. The detective's wife, a down-to-earth type Haley respected, kept a low profile, and their paths rarely crossed.

"Very much so," Mrs. Cluney answered softly.

So interesting how opposites attract, Haley thought.

An Officer Harris, who'd come alone, also sat with them. It was the first time Haley had had the pleasure of meeting the genial man.

"I'm surprised our paths haven't crossed before," Haley said. "I've had the pleasure of meeting many of Boston's finest."

"Well, at least now that's been rectified, Dr. Higgins. And the pleasure's all mine." He offered a hand. "Would you be so kind as to give me the next dance?"

Haley couldn't very well say no, but as she was seated across from Officer Harris, the man hadn't had a fair chance to judge her height. She, being tall for a woman, and he, on the short side for a man, had their coupling looking socially odd. They danced to "Dream a Little Dream of Me". Haley ignored the snickers that erupted around them, but poor Officer Harris looked distinctly perturbed. His lips pursed, causing his mustache to pucker like a hairy caterpillar, his eyes narrowed and hardened, and his palms began to sweat. They broke apart immediately upon the last note of the song.

"Thank you, Officer Harris," Haley said kindly. "You're a much better dancer than I."

Officer Harris could barely produce a smile. He

nodded and hurried back to his spot at the table. If Haley had been a betting gal, she would have bet ten bucks Officer Harris wished whiskey was legal.

SAMANTHA HAD NEVER BEEN to a policeman's ball. Marriage to Seth had them on opposite sides—cops were the enemy. They got in the way of all the illegal fun that Seth loved, like drinking, gambling, and yes, if Samantha were truthful, ladies of the night.

Tom was nothing like Seth, and despite herself, Samantha enjoyed his company. Where Seth was a brute, Tom was a gentleman. Where Seth talked about betting and where to get the best bootleg, Tom could carry on intelligent conversation. Where Seth was gruff, Tom was gentle.

Caution! Samantha thought. She might just fall for a cop!

"You look lovely," Tom said, as he spun her around, one hand clasping hers, the other on her waist.

"Thank you." Samantha had worn her dress before —a refurbished flapper dress she'd lengthened with new fringe on the hem and cinched with a belt when she'd chased a story at a speakeasy. Tom had seen her in it, being there on a case as well. Neither of them mentioned the fact.

They shared a table with two unmarried members of the force: Officer McAteer and Patrolman Fanning.

"Where'd you find this beauty, you ugly mutt?" Officer McAteer said with an appreciative head-to-toe appraisal of Samantha before she took her seat.

Patrolman Fanning joined in on the jesting. "Beauty and the Beast, hey?"

"Hey!" Samantha said. "Officer Bell is dashing!"

"Now I'm blushing," Tom said.

"But really," Officer McAteer pressed, "why haven't I seen you around, Miss Hawke."

"You probably will, now," Tom said. "Miss Hawke works for the *Boston Daily Record*. Just promoted from the ladies' pages."

Samantha held in the consternation she felt and couldn't help feeling defensive. "The ladies' pages are widely read, and advertisers pay a lot of dough for a spot. I still write them." She'd already taken plenty of photographs of the night's event. "Only now, I'm free to pursue other stories."

"Yeah?" the youthful patrolman said. "Are you working on a story now?"

"I'm following the death of the man at St. Stephen's Church. You wouldn't happen to know anything about that?"

Tom chuckled. "See? She's always on the job."

Samantha was serious. Tom didn't think she'd

agreed to be his date at the policeman's ball just to dance, did he? As much fun as it was, she wouldn't give up a night with Talia if it didn't mean there wasn't another possible payoff. Samantha pressed on. "It's so mysterious. He's still unidentified, or at least that's what your lot are leading the press to believe. Is it true? Why not surrender the name?"

Officer McAteer guffawed. "blond, beautiful, and a spitfire!"

"I'm only trying to do my job, Officer," Samantha returned stiffly. "The same as you, when you're on duty."

Realizing she had yet to use the best of her feminine wiles, Samantha shifted in her chair and crossed her legs, allowing her calf to show. She smiled and batted lashes that were thick with mascara. "Does one of you fine gentlemen have a cigarette you could spare?"

Both Officer McAteer and Patrolman Fanning whipped out cigarette cases from their pockets. Officer McAteer, being closer, handed Samantha a cigarette, then leaned over with a lighter. Samantha took a long, and what she hoped was seductive, pull on the ciggie.

"Thanks, Officer."

Tom Bell cleared his throat, the joy from his normally friendly expression gone. "Can I get you a drink, Samantha?"

"That would be the cat's meow," she said. "Cola would be nice."

Tom strutted away from the table, and Samantha made her move on the two men. She leaned forward on her elbows and let a tiny bit of cleavage show.

"If you had a little tip you could give me, I'd be ever so grateful."

The two men shared a look. Officer McAteer gave a subtle shake of the head.

"So sorry, Miss Hawke," Officer Fanning said. "We wish we could help, but unfortunately, we're just as much in the dark as you. As you know, most murder cases are never solved."

Samantha squashed the remainder of her cigarette in the ashtray in a fit of dismay. Foiled again.

3

The next day at work, Samantha couldn't help but feel anxious about not making any strides on the church body case. What kind of investigative reporter was she, anyway? It didn't help that she had to submit this story on the policemen's ball before Mr. August would release her to focus on other things.

The ball itself was a standard social event's reporting affair. Who attended, who wore what dress, what the food and music were like. Samantha studied the photographs she'd developed that morning. She'd gone around to each table, introduced herself, and taken a photo. Her own table appeared to be the most camera shy. Both Officer McAteer and Patrolman Fanning had looked away when she'd snapped, which caused her to capture their blurry profiles. Only Tom looked boldly at her lens and smiled.

Among the roomful of policemen were a handful of female police officers. Samantha had spoken in length with one and thought she'd make an interesting feature for the ladies' pages.

"What are you working on?"

Samantha's gaze darted up from her typewriter at the sound of Johnny's voice.

"The policeman's ball, if you must know." She threw the question back. "What are you working on?"

He shrugged, and Samantha started typing again and fumed at the way information seemed to travel one way.

"Rough business on the docks," Johnny finally offered. "Did you go with a date?"

Samantha stilled. "Huh?"

"To the ball," Johnny said. "Did you go on a date or on assignment?"

"Can't I do both?"

"So, you did go on a date. Not that dainty Bell fellow?"

"He's not *dainty*," Samantha spat. "Tom's as rugged as they come."

"So, it's Tom now, is it?"

"Yes, *Johnny*, it's Tom. Now, if you don't mind, I'm writing a piece on Irene McAuliffe."

"The first woman to join the Boston police department." Johnny snorted. "Blah, blah, blah."

Samantha stared at her coworker with indignation. "There were very few female police officers represented last night. If the piece inspires more women to join the force, then I've done my job."

"How many women police officers do you think it takes to protect the young ladies of Boston from attention from the opposite sex?"

"They do a lot more than monitor the comings and goings of young women. Margaret Foley—"

"I know," Johnny said, cutting her off. "She was the first woman to arrest an armed criminal. An outlier. Hardly the norm."

"The norm can be changed."

Samantha pushed away from her desk. She needed a cup of tea and regretted that nothing stronger was on offer.

SAMANTHA WORKED HARD to keep her biggest secret —she and her family were dirt poor and lived in a tenement building. If it weren't for her job at the paper, she, her daughter, and mother-in-law would be the widows and orphans that charities looked after.

The stench of communal living never dulled, and the first few seconds after coming in from the fresh outdoor air was always a bit of a shock. Samantha pushed through the disagreeable smell of burned toast and greasy sausages and headed to her second-floor apartment. A baby cried, and a radio show could be heard from down the hall. Samantha got her key ready, opened the scarred door, and stepped inside.

"Mommy!"

This was Samantha's favorite moment of each day, and she relished the feeling of the small girl who ran into her arms. One day, in the far-too-near future, Talia would suddenly stop running to greet her, and Samantha's heart already hurt at the thought. She wished there was a way she could spend more time with her daughter, but life's demands just got in the way.

"Hey, honey," Samantha said. "How was your day?"

"It was okay."

Samantha dropped her messenger bag and camera into the corner and removed her hat and summer gloves. From the living room, with its sparse furnishings and aged wallpaper, she could see the simple wooden table and chair set in the small kitchen.

Bina, with her thin arms propped in sharp angles on her narrow waist, stared across the living room disapprovingly. "It's not too late for me to warm up a pot of stew."

"Dr. Higgins is expecting us."

Bina wrung her hands. "Then we'll have to return the invitation. Have you thought of that? Do you really want to have your fancy doctor friend see where you live? Like pigs in a sty!"

Bina exaggerated, but she had a point, and one Samantha had thought long and hard about. She planned to invite Haley and her house companion, Miss McPhail, out for a picnic. What else could she do? She and Haley had forged a friendship over the summer, and Samantha had refused one invitation. To say no a second time would be offensive, and Samantha didn't want to risk losing Haley as a friend. Not only were their jobs compatible, each at times providing information the other needed, but Samantha liked Haley. Working long hours at the paper kept her from making relationships with other women her age, most of whom were married and homemakers. And if Bina ended up being the only adult female in her life, Samantha would go nuts.

Samantha held her tongue and took Talia by the hand. "Let's get ready. Do you remember that I told you Dr. Higgins has a cat?"

"Only three legs," Talia said. "That's sad."

"Don't let Mr. Midnight hear you say that. I doubt he even knows he's supposed to have four."

The apartment had only two bedrooms, which

meant Samantha shared with her daughter. She didn't mind. Talia's angelic presence while sleeping was a blessing and joy, and preferable to the steam-engine snoring and cigarette breath she'd endured when Seth was around.

Samantha didn't have a large wardrobe and only a couple of dresses that were too fancy for work— remnants from the shorter, square cuts of the twenties. Samantha's thrifty alterations were common among the frugal, and she'd even written about the tips in the ladies' pages, and had gotten many thankful letters in reply.

After brushing and repinning her short curls behind her ears, Samantha slipped into a dress and studied herself in the mirror.

"You look pretty, Mommy."

Samantha smiled at Talia's reflection. "Thank you, honey. Now, let me brush your hair."

When they were finished getting ready, they found Bina at the kitchen table, still wearing her day frock with a spotted apron tied on, with a defiant look on her face.

"Bina?" Samantha said. "You need to get ready. We have to leave soon, or we're going to be late." Samantha wanted to catch the bus as a taxi, especially at this busy time of day, would be too expensive.

"*Feh*! I'm not going. I told you already. If you want me to meet your fancy friends, then you have to move us somewhere nicer."

Bina had lived in the tenement building since she and her late husband had immigrated from Europe, and hadn't complained—as much—until most of the Jewish families had moved south, and Italian immigrants had taken their places.

"This is as nice as it's going to get," Samantha snapped, then, after a long exhale, added, "Fine, Talia and I will go without you."

Bina's head snapped up.

Did she think Samantha would cancel because the older woman put her heels in? Samantha was honestly relieved. At least now, she wouldn't have to be on pins and needles all evening out of fear that Bina would say something offensive.

Standing at the mirror by the door, Samantha pinned on a small felt hat adorned with a decorative ribbon and meant to be worn at an angle, and then pulled on a pair of cotton gloves. She reached for her daughter.

"Come on, Talia."

Before heading out of the door, Samantha checked the pockets of her dress again. The scrap of paper she'd nicked from the church body was inside one. Before the night was over, Samantha would have to come clean with Haley. Her friend might be angry or disappointed by what Samantha had done, but Samantha was sure Haley would be grateful to see the contents of the note before the police did.

4

———

*H*aley had learned over the years that the best way to help Molly in the kitchen was to stay out of her way. Her companion, who'd come from sturdy Irish stock, was proficient in the kitchen, and a good conservationist. Haley could hardly imagine life without her.

Once Haley had set the table, her aid was done until the meal was over, and it was time for cleanup. The scent of roast and potatoes caused Haley to salivate, and she escaped to her home office to distract herself with work.

Haley's office was her refuge. Furnished with a lovely oak desk, a comfortable chair, and a shelf full of books, it was a place where Haley could relax. Or think. Or both. A golf putting mat along the window called to her, and she picked up her putter propped in the corner, set a golf ball on a tee, and set about concentrating on the shot.

She thought about the John Doe, and for a moment, regretted that Samantha and her family were coming. She really wanted to go back to the church and take another look around. Maybe someone who lived nearby had seen something.

Her distraction caused her to miss her shot, and the little white ball veered off the green mat and onto the hardwood floor.

She glanced out the window onto Grove Street as she retrieved her wayward ball. An inheritance, clever investing, and foresight to pull her money out of the market before the crash had enabled Haley to purchase her plush apartment and to set aside a nice nest egg for the future. She'd been fortunate in this regard and didn't take it for granted. She was grateful not to have to depend on a man or even her job for financial security.

The door of the office pushed open and Haley heard a quiet meow. Mr. Midnight was banished from the kitchen when Molly was busy, a fact he didn't like. He hobbled on his three legs to Haley's side, and Haley swooped him into her arms.

"I know you're not used to children, Mr. Midnight,

but I hope you'll be on your best behavior when our guests arrive."

Out the window four floors below, Haley spotted Samantha step off a bus with a young child in tow. Haley had met the little girl before, but the mother-in-law, Mrs. Rosenbaum, remained a mystery. Samantha had relayed several funny stories about her life with her absentee husband's mother, and Haley was eager to put a face to the character.

Haley frowned. From what she could see, Samantha had arrived with only her daughter. The duo disappeared into the building, and Haley, with Mr. Midnight in her arms, went to the front door to wait for Samantha to knock.

Just off the entrance, a set of double glass doors was propped open to the living room. It was a comfortable space with a high ceiling and tall windows to let in natural light. The walls were papered in a rich burgundy floral pattern, and the furniture facing a fireplace had complementary upholstery with ornate wood trim.

The anticipated knock occurred. Haley shouted over her shoulder for Molly's benefit, "They're here," then opened the door.

Samantha and her daughter looked so much alike with their honey-blond hair and blue eyes, Haley couldn't help but break into a wide smile.

"Come in," she said eagerly. She bent to Talia's level and stroked Mr. Midnight's black head. "Hi. I'm Dr. Higgins. Do you like cats?"

Talia pressed into her mother's leg.

"She's shy," Samantha explained.

Molly appeared and offered to take their summer coats.

"Molly, this is Talia," Haley said. "Talia, this is Miss McPhail."

When introductions had been completed, Haley invited Samantha and Talia into the living room. "Would you like a glass of lemonade?" she asked. "Molly makes the best, with fresh lemons and a lot of sugar."

Talia snuggled on the settee beside her mother and nodded.

"Thank you, Haley," Samantha said. "That would be lovely."

Haley returned with a tray of glasses and found Samantha looking at one of her framed Higgins family photos.

"These are your brothers," Samantha stated.

"Yes." Haley pointed to the one standing next to her. "That's Joe."

Samantha glanced up at Haley with a look of understanding. "He was a handsome man."

Mr. Midnight hopped onto the settee beside Talia. The little girl tentatively touched the feline's head.

"How did he lose his leg, Dr. Higgins?" the little girl asked.

"We don't actually know." Haley handed out the lemonade and then sat in one of the chairs. "Miss McPhail found him at the fire escape door off the kitchen. It was the middle of the night, so she dubbed him Mr. Midnight for the timing of his arrival and for the fact that his fur is very black."

"He's nice," Talia said, after a sip.

Haley grinned at the cat. "I think he likes you."

"Thank you again for inviting us," Samantha said. "I'm sorry my mother-in-law couldn't make it. She's unwell."

Haley caught the warning-to-stay-quiet look Samantha shot at her daughter and chose not to intrude. "I'm sorry to hear it. Maybe another time."

Samantha nodded but didn't commit.

Molly called them in for supper. As per usual, everything was exquisite from the decor on the table to the orchestra playing on the radio.

"Shall we give thanks?" Molly said.

This was the awkward part, Haley thought. Molly was Irish and a devout Catholic, Haley tended to the unpopular agnostic position—she just wasn't certain where her beliefs landed regarding religion—and

Samantha, born a protestant, had married into the Jewish culture. What a mix!

"Please," Samantha said. "How you normally do would be wonderful."

Everyone lowered their heads and clasped their hands as Molly prayed. "Bless us, O Lord, and these thy gifts which we are about to receive from thy bounty, through Christ our Lord. Amen."

Haley had opened an eye to peek at her guests. While Samantha had kept her eyes sealed, little Talia did just the opposite, staring wide-eyed at Molly—especially when she performed the sign of the cross. Haley bit her lip to keep from smiling inappropriately.

Molly passed the platter of meat. "It's beef," she said, unnecessarily, but Haley knew Molly was concerned about keeping the entire meal kosher.

"How sad Mrs. Rosenbaum couldn't make it," Molly said. "I'm sure she could've given me tips on how to better prepare brisket."

"If this is your first try," Samantha said after a bite, "then you're a natural."

If Talia hadn't been in the party, Haley would've broken out one of her contraband brandies. Molly was European, and Haley had lived many years in Europe where drinking wine with a meal was as common as water. They both thought prohibition was nonsense.

However, it was still against the law, and Haley

only brought the spirits out occasionally. She and Samantha had shared a glass once over the summer, and it was a secret that somehow bonded them, despite their social differences.

"How is school, Talia?" Haley asked.

Talia's sweet countenance darkened. "It's okay."

Samantha had confided in Haley that Talia was being picked on at school for being part Jewish. Haley raised a brow in question. Samantha nodded sadly, "It's still going on. She doesn't like to talk about it."

"We will change the subject then," Haley said. "What's your favorite book?"

Talia cheered. "*Anne of Green Gables!*"

"Oh, I love those books," Molly said. "I own every one!"

Talia glanced at Samantha under long eyelashes, then said, "We get our books from the library."

"Marvelous! We're so fortunate to have a terrific library in Boston. What about games?"

"I like Tiddlywinks."

"How serendipitous," Molly said. "I have that very game in the cupboard. Maybe the two of us could play a game later?"

Haley adored Molly! Samantha had mentioned Talia's affection for Tiddlywinks, so Haley had asked Molly to make a purchase, but she hadn't expected her companion to offer to entertain the girl. It was a perfect plan because Haley had an idea.

"Maybe, while you two are playing, Samantha and I could go for a little ride in the DeSoto."

Samantha seemed to read Haley's mind. "Good idea. Hanover Street?"

5

"I'm amazed that Talia was willing to stay behind without me," Samantha said, looking over at Haley.

"It's Molly. And Mr. Midnight. They're an irresistible combination." Haley drove her DeSoto east toward Hanover Street. "I think we're in time to catch the tail end of mass."

Samantha smirked. "Are you considering converting?"

"Not tonight. I'm hoping we can find someone who might have seen something suspicious. At the very least, I'd like to have another look around. I find nosing about a little disconcerting when Detective Cluney is watching," Haley replied.

"He's a bit protective of his territory, isn't he?" Samantha said.

"I imagine that's true of us all," Haley answered. "He's just doing his job."

"And what are you doing?" Samantha said as Haley parked.

Haley chuckled. "I guess I'm also trying to do his job."

Samantha understood what made Haley go beyond the line of duty when it came to the dead bodies lying in the morgue. It had everything to do with Haley's brother and Haley's inability to solve the case. Doing for others what she couldn't do for Joe Higgins was what drove her. Murder is wrong, and justice is the only answer.

After coming to a stop, Samantha said, "Before we go inside, I have a confession to make."

Haley raised a dark brow. "Isn't that a job for Father O'Hara?"

"Haha. No, I'm serious. I did something you're not going to approve of, and just, in my defense, I want to say that it was an impulsive gesture on my part. I didn't have a chance to think it through."

"Okay, now I'm worried."

Samantha sighed and removed the piece of paper from her pocket. "I took this from the suit pocket of your John Doe."

Haley stared back in disbelief. "You're right. I don't approve."

"It was sticking out, and my instincts as a reporter kicked in. I was only going to read it and put it back before Mr. Mulryan returned from calling the police."

"But?"

"But then I read it."

Samantha held out the folded scrap of paper. "I thought you'd want to see it."

Haley hesitated. "You should give it to the police."

"I know I should. And I will. But trust me. You want to know what's written there."

Haley held out an open palm and then read the notation.

Watch your foul mouth, or you'll end up like Higgins.

Haley gasped and stared back at Samantha. "This was on our John Doe?"

"Right suit pocket." Samantha felt bad about inflicting any pain on her friend. "You know, it's probably just a coincidence. Higgins is a common name."

Haley blankly stared ahead for a few moments before speaking. "I haven't shown you the police photos I have of Joe. He was lying, twisted on his side."

"The photographs I snapped at the crime scene were similar to Joe's?"

Haley nodded once.

"I think this John Doe knew my brother, and whatever they were involved in, it got them both killed."

"Any ideas?" Samantha asked.

Haley deftly slipped the note into her purse and shook her head. "Let's go inside."

THE FRONT DOORS OF ST. Stephen's church were wide open due to the lingering heat of the day, and, from behind, parishioners could be seen seated while Father O'Hara stood on the podium.

Samantha had a foot on the first step when she realized Haley hadn't joined her but instead had headed around the side of the building to where the body had been found. Samantha hurried to catch up.

She found Haley nibbling her lower lip as she scanned the area with dark eyes. Samantha followed her gaze, wondering what Haley was looking for and what the doctor could see that Samantha couldn't, beyond drying-out grass and clumps of weeds growing along the foundation.

To Samantha's astonishment, Haley drew out a magnifying glass from her purse, tugged on her slacks, and squatted. Systematically, she scoured the area where the body had lain.

"What are you doing?" Samantha asked.

"Looking for trace evidence. Somebody dropped the body, and maybe that somebody left something behind."

Samantha watched with interest as Haley produced a pair of tweezers and plucked what looked like a piece of dried mud off the lawn.

"Dirt?" she asked.

"Yes, but what kind?" Haley said. "It looks like harbor muck. There's nothing like it on this sod. Could've come from the bottom of the killer's shoe." Haley retrieved a small paper bag and dropped the clay bit into it. Samantha wondered what else Haley carried in her purse.

When Samantha and Haley finally entered the church, they slipped into an empty pew at the back. The priest said the benediction prayer then, with a train of boys dressed in white cloaks behind him, headed down the middle aisle to the front door.

Congregants genuflected, a bend in the knee as they faced the golden embossed tabernacle before filing quietly out of the church. Samantha recognized Mrs. Breen, who'd stopped within hearing distance to gossip with a group of gray-haired ladies.

"I knew instantly that he was dead," Mrs. Breen said. "With the blood on his neck and the fact he wasn't breathing."

One lady responded with a deep look of concern. "How awful, Doreen. You'll have nightmares."

"Oh, I doubt that," Mrs. Breen said. "I know you have trouble sleeping, Ethel, but I sleep like a baby."

The older ladies took their commiserating outside.

Samantha nudged Haley and lifted her chin. "Mr. Mulryan appears to be having a serious chat with that tall gentleman."

Haley hummed. "Let's draw closer."

The men huddled in, their backs toward Haley and Samantha as they quietly approached.

"I told you I'd get you the money," Mr. Mulryan insisted.

The stranger replied calmly, "You've got two days." He placed his hat on his head and turned, nearly running into Samantha.

"Oh, hi there," he said with a smile. Samantha was used to appreciative looks from the opposite sex. Her blond locks tended to catch the eye, both a blessing and a curse. She batted her eyes. "Hello, Mr.—"

"Delaney." The man removed his hat. "Are you new to St. Stephen's? I think I would've remembered seeing you."

"Just visiting," Samantha said. "I'm here with my friend, Dr. Higgins."

Mr. Delaney raised a brow in interest. "A lady doctor?"

"A pathologist, actually," Haley stated proudly. "And assistant medical examiner. I'd like to have a word with Mr. Mulryan. I hope we didn't interrupt."

Mr. Delaney's eyes darkened as he placed his hat

on his head once again. "Not at all. I was just leaving. It's been a pleasure to meet you both." He strutted out without looking back, and Samantha couldn't help but shiver. Mr. Delaney was the type of man whose bad side was probably atrocious.

Mr. Mulryan stared at Mr. Delaney until the man disappeared from the church. His skin was pale, and he plucked a handkerchief from his cotton suit pocket and patted at the sweat droplets that had appeared on his long forehead. "If you're here about the body," he said, "I've already told the police everything I know."

"Are you sure you didn't recognize the victim?" Haley asked.

"No. I've already said so many times."

"Is Mr. Delaney a regular attender?" Haley continued.

"Sometimes," the secretary struggled to keep his impatience at bay. "Not always. Now, I don't understand the meaning of this questioning. I need to attend to church matters."

6

*H*aley had never had the chance to examine the spot where her brother's body had been discovered. She'd received word of his murder while living in London. By the time she'd returned to Boston, any trace evidence that might've been found had long since been trampled upon, blown away, or dissolved in the rain. Having made it back from London just in time for the funeral, she'd only seen Joe's body after it had been cleaned up and embalmed and was lying in a coffin. The bruises on his face and hands had been covered with makeup and the injury to his neck hidden by a high-collared shirt and black tie.

"Hey, Doc." Mr. Martin joined Haley in the morgue where she was positioned over a microscope. "What's up?"

"It's a piece of clay I found where our John Doe was dropped. I think the killer might've dragged it there."

"A piece of dirt?"

"Yes. A piece of dirt. It was out of place on the sod, which was also dried out, but clearly topsoil." Haley sighed. She knew this was a long shot, but it was a *shot*, at least, one she hadn't got with Joe.

"And?" Mr. Martin prompted.

"With its silty, hardened appearance, it looks like it may be from the harbor. I'm going to send it to the laboratory to confirm."

"So—"

"If we can determine where this piece of clay came from, we might be able to find the scene of the crime," Haley said. "At least narrow it down, anyway."

"The riverbank is a long stretch," Mr. Martin added—quite unhelpfully, Haley thought.

Dr. Guthrie meandered out of his office and stared Haley's way with a look of indecision on his face. "Dr. Higgins, might I have a word." His bushy white eyebrows darted in Mr. Martin's direction, making it clear that whatever he had to say was for Haley's ears only.

She felt a shot of worry. Had Mr. Martin done something her boss objected to? She hoped not. It wasn't that easy to find a competent intern, and Haley had spent valuable time training him. Then again, she couldn't expect Mr. Martin to stay forever.

Was it her, then? Had Detective Cluney called? Maybe Mr. Mulryan had filed a complaint about her brash questions from the evening before. It wouldn't be the first time the detective had got into a flap about her "infringing on police business", but he usually took his beef directly to her. If he'd by-stepped to Dr. Guthrie, then the detective was really put out.

"Dr. Guthrie?" Haley started as they moved into the man's office. "Is something wrong?"

"What? No, no. Have a seat. No, don't bother, this won't take a minute."

Her curiosity roused, Haley waited. "Yes?"

Dr. Guthrie swallowed. "Has Mol—Miss McPhail, has she mentioned. . . anything?"

Good heavens. Dr. Guthrie, with his mop of wavy white hair, blistering blue eyes behind crinkled skin, pointy knees and elbows, and an Oxford degree, was consulting Haley on matters of the *heart*. She knew that Molly and Dr. Guthrie had struck up a friendship a while back, had shared a breakfast or two together, but then it appeared that interest had faded. At least for Molly. Her companion hadn't mentioned Dr. Guthrie in some time.

That was odd, now that Haley thought about it. Molly loved to discuss Haley's work with her over their evening meal. How had they continued to do that without speaking of the chief pathologist?

"Mentioned what, Doctor?"

Dr. Guthrie had all the finesse of an awkward teenager. "Do you think . . . it's just that. . . well, our last encounter didn't go. . . And I wondered if—"

Haley came to his rescue. "Would you like me to give Miss McPhail a message on your behalf?"

"Would you?"

"Of course."

"Very well then." Dr. Guthrie held his chin as he paced in front of his desk. "Tell her, I regret being insensitive...no, I'm sorry for not... no—"

"Maybe you should write it down," Haley suggested.

"Yes, you're right." Dr. Guthrie scratched his head. "Thank you, Dr. Higgins."

Haley bit the inside of her lip as she returned to her desk. This side of Dr. Guthrie was endearing.

"What's so funny?" Mr. Martin said.

"Oh, nothing. Dr. Guthrie just needed some advice. Now, if you think you can hold the fort, I have a few errands I'd like to run."

"I'll keep it afloat, Doctor."

"Thank you, Mr. Martin."

Haley grabbed her hat, gloves, and the folded copy of the *Boston Daily Record* sitting on her desk, and left.

· · ·

HALEY LIVED CLOSE ENOUGH to the hospital that she often walked, but today, because of early morning rain, she'd driven her DeSoto, which was serendipitous as she now needed it.

She considered herself fortunate, as a female, to even own her own car—something that most American women could only aspire to. If they were lucky, their husbands owned one and would let them drive, but it was rare to see a broad-brimmed hat behind the wheel.

Hanover Street, once a billboard of prosperity and opportunity, now had dirty-faced men sitting idly against the corners of brick buildings where they smoked cigarettes and looked worried. By noon, the soup line on Huntington would snake several blocks, and Haley despaired for what would happen to the homeless in the brutal winters so typical of Boston.

Parking in front of the *Boston Daily Record*, Haley clasped her purse and went inside.

The receptionist, a middle-aged lady lacking a wedding band—*much like herself*, Haley thought— greeted her cordially.

"I'd like to see Miss Hawke," Haley said. "If she's in. Please tell her it's Dr. Higgins."

The receptionist's eyes rounded at the news of Haley's title, a common response by most of those who didn't know her, then did Haley's bidding. Shortly afterward, Samantha breezed into the lobby. "Haley, what a surprise!" She lowered her voice and added, "And a breath of fresh air. Good grief, I'm sick of working with men all the time."

Haley laughed, then said, "Can I treat you to lunch? It's work related if that makes a difference."

"I'm sure I can sneak away. Mr. August is demanding, but he doesn't require me to starve. I'll just grab my things."

Haley grabbed Samantha's arm. "Also, I was wondering about the photographs—"

"Yes," Samantha said knowingly. "I'll bring them along."

They'd just gotten comfortable in Haley's car when Johnny Milwaukee's fingers gripped the edge of Samantha's open window. "Hello, lovely ladies."

"We're just going for lunch, Johnny," Samantha said. "Don't worry. I'm not trying to scoop you."

Haley smirked. Journalists had their own versions of the truth.

"I'm not accusing you of anything, doll," Johnny said.

Haley would've sworn that the cocky man's eyes twinkled. He tapped the hood of the DeSoto. "Have fun!"

Samantha scowled, and Haley chuckled.

"What's so funny?" Samantha said. "The man's a menace."

"I think you like him."

"I do not!"

Haley pinched her lips together, and Samantha protested again. "Seriously, Johnny Milwaukee gets under my skin. He's arrogant, conceited, uh . . ."

"Attractive, funny, smart."

Samantha seared Haley with a look. "Maybe I'm not the one who likes him."

Haley chuckled lightly. "Stand down, soldier. Anyway, I didn't pick you up to talk about your colleagues." Haley pulled onto a side street in front of one of her favorite coffee shops. "Have you eaten here before?"

Samantha shook her head. Haley wasn't surprised. Samantha's financial burdens weren't enviable, and if there was one thing Haley had learned about her new friend, it was that she was frugal.

"They have great Reubens," Haley added.

"I don't like sauerkraut," Samantha said, still pouting.

"How about turkey?"

Samantha sighed. "Yes, thanks. Sorry for my moods. Johnny's a rat, but I shouldn't take my frustration out on you."

"It's okay," Haley said. "I probably deserved it."

The coffee shop was a long and narrow "hole in the wall" with red vinyl booths along one side and a row of chrome stools parallel with a counter on the other. Haley and Samantha claimed the last empty booth.

When the waitress arrived, Haley ordered a Reuben on rye for herself and a turkey and Swiss for Samantha. "My tab," she added.

"That's really not necessary," Samantha said, but Haley suspected otherwise.

"I asked you because I want something from you."

"The photographs of the crime scene."

"Yes."

"I thought you were chummy with one of the police photographers?"

Haley lifted a shoulder. "I'm pushing the line with Detective Cluney. He doesn't like me nosing in on his cases."

Samantha scoffed. "Even though you're the one that solves them most of the time?"

"Not most of the time," Haley replied humbly. "Some of the time. Anyway, can I see them?"

Samantha removed the large manila envelope from her messenger bag. "Johnny caught sight of these, but I stopped him from getting a good look. I told you he was a pain in the *derrière*. Excuse my French."

Haley grinned then pulled the prints out of the

envelope, but before she could have a look, the waitress returned with a pot of steaming coffee."

"Coffee, ladies?"

Both Haley and Samantha pushed white mugs toward the server, and she poured.

"Cream and sugar are on the table."

Haley motioned for Samantha to go first, and she made a second attempt at viewing the photos. The images made her blood grow cold.

"Something wrong?" Samantha asked.

Haley pulled an envelope out of her oversized purse, removed a photograph, and handed it to Samantha.

"That's Joe."

"Oh. Yes. I see the similarities." Samantha could sense the weight of Haley's sorrow and she knew nothing she could say would make things better. With a gentle look she said simply, "I'm sorry for your loss."

"Thank you." Haley brushed a curl off her face. "I know it's been a while since Joe's been gone, but sometimes it feels like it just happened yesterday." She smiled weakly. "The human psyche is so fragile."

Samantha returned the photograph and changed the subject back to the case at hand. "What did you find out about your tiny piece of clay?"

"I'm pretty sure it's from the riverbank. I've sent it to the laboratory for confirmation."

Like Mr. Martin before her, Samantha relayed the obvious. "The riverbank's a long piece of real estate."

"Yes, but it's smaller than the whole of Boston."

Their meals arrived, and Haley felt a little concerned at the aggressive way in which Samantha attacked her sandwich. On closer look, Samantha did appear rather thin. Such was the sign of the times.

Once her initial stab of hunger appeared to have abated, Samantha asked, "Did you notice anything in my photographs? Something I've missed?"

"See that bit of white sticking out of the pocket?"

"Oh, yeah, the note."

"I wouldn't show the police these. They wouldn't match up with the ones Jack took."

"Jack?" Samantha wiggled a brow. "You're on first-name basis, are you now?"

"We've been friends for a while." Haley would not say more about that.

Samantha took the hint. "I didn't notice the note until after I shot the photographs. I knew I didn't have a lot of time. Mrs. Breen only stepped away for a few minutes, and then Mr. Mulryan came back."

Haley hummed. "There's something about Mr. Mulryan that doesn't sit right with me."

Samantha agreed. "He certainly acted suspiciously. Not exactly pals with Mr. Delaney."

"Yet close enough to get reprimanded by him."

"What does Mr. Delaney do, I wonder?" Samantha asked.

"That's a good question. How would a person find out?"

Samantha blew through pursed lips. "I have a contact at the paper who knows everything and everyone in Boston." She snorted with derision.

"Let me guess," Haley said. "Johnny Milwaukee."

7

The bull pit was in an uproar when Samantha returned to her desk after lunch with Haley. Telephones rang, the telegram rumbled, and bells clanged as madmen got to the end of the line on their typewriters and beat the level to push the roller back into place. Samantha, once again, felt behind the eight ball.

"What happened?" Samantha said, dismayed. "What'd I miss?"

Johnny looked up from his typewriter. "Babe Ruth just hit his six hundredth home run."

Samantha wrinkled her nose. *That was it?* "All this excitement's over baseball?"

"It's not just baseball, doll, it's Babe Ruth. He's somethin'!"

Samantha removed her hat and gloves and settled

into her chair. "Plays for New York, right?"

"Sure, but he's a Boston boy. Played here first. Damn shame they sold him."

Samantha shrugged. "Maybe they'll buy him back one day."

Johnny leaned back in his chair, cigarette in hand, and put his feet up on his desk. "Now, there's an idea!" He kept his gaze locked on Samantha. She knew he got a kick out of making her uneasy, and she could never tell for sure if his interest in her was purely professional or not. Either way, it hadn't stopped him from asking her out on more than one occasion. She prided herself that she'd said no to him every time, except for when it benefited her job as an investigative reporter.

This time she took the initiative and sauntered over to his desk. His eyes—quite handsome, Samantha had to admit—widened in surprise when she propped herself on the edge of his desk.

"Are you going to ask me out?" Johnny said with a sly glance.

"No. But I do have a question for you."

"Shoot."

"Do you know a Mr. Mulryan? He's the secretary at St. Stephen's church."

"You nosing about in that murder?"

"And if I am?"

"I want in?"

"In how? And no, this is my story."

"Then, sorry, I don't know him."

"Johnny!"

"Sorry, doll. This is how the game works. I give a little, you give a little."

"Fine."

"Fine, what?"

"We can share the byline, but only if you do your share in breaking the story. I'm not gonna do all the work and give you half the glory."

Johnny let his feet fall to the floor and held out a hand, insisting they shake on it.

"Partners."

"Not partners." She shook his hand. "Just coworkers on this case. And my name goes first. Now, what do you know?"

"Mulryan's known to the police."

Samantha scowled. She knew the police knew Mr. Mulryan. She'd been there when they questioned him.

"I mean, he's been arrested before. Gambling."

Samantha thought about the terse conversation between Mulryan and Delaney. "What kind of gambling?"

"That's the bit that's tough to break. Underground fight clubs. They move from location to location and, word has it, there are dirty coppers involved that help keep it hidden."

"Do you know a fellow named Delaney?"

Johnny smiled crookedly with a look of admiration. "Look at who's the newshound. William Delaney's a rumored organizer of the fights. How do you know about him?"

"He was at mass last night. I overheard him talking with Mulryan. It sounded like a threat. Mulryan owes him money."

"See? Gambling."

"What else do you know? Did you recognize the body?"

"Didn't see the face. Cluney's as tight as a drum when it comes to information. My contact at the station says he's keeping info close to his chest. You know what that means?"

"It's a big story?"

"That's right, doll. It's a big story." Johnny leaned in, stubbed out his cigarette, then said, "You got pictures?"

"Why would I have pictures?"

Johnny pointed to his temple with a long finger. "Cuz, you were there covering a ladies' thing. Had your little camera with you. Guarded the darkroom like a mama bear with cubs."

"Fine. I do."

"If you show them to me, I might be able to tell you who the unlucky guy is."

"If you can do that, so can the cops."

Johnny held out his palms. "Fine. Go talk to the cops."

Samantha sighed. If she wanted Johnny to play fair with her, she needed to do the same for him. She stepped back to her desk and waved him over. Removing the manila envelope from her messenger bag, she pulled out the top photograph with a close-up of the face. The twisted way the body was dumped was a detail she planned to keep to herself. At least for now.

Johnny emitted a low grumble.

"Do you know him?"

"He looks an awful lot like Sean Keating, but I don't think it's him."

"Why not?"

"Because Keating died in a cocaine raid a year ago. I covered the story."

BOSTON HAD ETHNIC QUARTERS, and the largest one in the North End was Little Italy. According to the residential files collected by the paper over the years there were five Irish families with the name Keating in the area. With only the patriarch's name listed, Samantha had no way to find out if any of these people were related to Sean Keating, and if they were missing a family member. Chances were high that the cops had figured out the identification already, but if they had, they hadn't put out an official announcement to the press.

Samantha lifted the receiver of her standard black telephone, a new introduction to her desk—a reward of sorts for showing her mettle when she'd broken the last big story. Without hesitation, she dialed the morgue.

"Please connect me to Dr. Higgins."

Samantha turned her back to the room, and especially to Johnny, as she waited for Haley to answer.

"Hello, Haley," she said once Haley was connected, "It's Samantha. I think Johnny came through, though I had to make a deal with the devil to get him to talk. He says our guy looks like another guy who kicked the dust last year, a man named Sean Keating."

"A brother to our John Doe," Haley said. "Or a cousin?"

"That's my thinking. There are five Keating families in South Boston, but I don't know if it's worth trying to call. Have you heard anything from your cop friend?"

"Nothing. It's like they're trying to keep news of the death under wraps."

Samantha's spine tingled with the growing belief she might be sitting on a huge story. She and Johnny, that was.

"Should we go door to door?" Samantha asked. "I have the addresses."

"Let me take a look at the morgue files first," Haley said. "We have information on pretty much every family in the city, at least those who've lost a family member in the last fifty years."

"Why do you think the police are keeping mum," Samantha asked. "Johnny suggested dirty cops."

"I hope not, though it's hard to imagine a perfectly aboveboard station house. Why don't you contact Officer Bell? Maybe he'll feed you a nibble."

"He was my next call. You should know that Johnny said Delaney is organizing fight clubs around the city. They move around, which makes them hard to track."

"That doesn't surprise me," Haley said. "And I bet it's safe to say, Mr. Mulryan is involved somehow."

"At least as a gambler." Samantha clicked her tongue. "He doesn't look like much of a fighter."

"I've read about William Delaney," Haley said. "I didn't put it together at first, but he owns several apartments and tenements in the city."

Samantha felt her cheeks warm. How could she have missed that? Her own building was owned by an elusive businessman with the name William Delaney.

"What are you going to do now?" Samantha asked.

"I'm going search my files for information on the

family name of Keating, and then take a drive through South Boston. Should I pick you up?"

"I'll be waiting."

Samantha hung up and risked a look at Johnny, who looked back with questioning eyes. "That was Dr. Higgins. She's going to check the morgue files on Keating."

The morsel seemed to satisfy him. Samantha had no time to waste. Unlike the men in the room, she had to keep up with the ladies' pages alongside other newsworthy leads. It was the deal Archie August had made with her if she wanted more leash.

She'd written up the church fundraiser as if a dead body hadn't marred it and focused on the social side of the story and the efforts of the volunteers. Matching it up with a life tip seemed like a good idea. She searched the ladies' magazines—an expense Mr. August had approved so she could research for the columns—and found a recipe for making toothpaste. It was okay to copy the information, using her own words, so long as she mentioned her original source.

All it takes is sea salt, baking soda, and peppermint.

After a short while, Samantha heard the faint sound of three short blasts from a car horn. Without looking at Johnny, she grabbed her things and hurried outside. She pretended not to hear him when he shouted, "Hey, Sam!"

Just as she climbed into Haley's car, she caught sight of a man hovering around the corner. She could've sworn it was Seth.

8

————

*H*aley watched with amusement as Samantha ran out the front doors of the *Boston Daily Record* building.

"Is it on fire?" she said as Samantha jumped into the DeSoto.

"Just go. I don't want Johnny to follow."

Samantha stared over her shoulder, and Haley wondered if her friend was a little paranoid.

Haley pulled into traffic. "What makes you think Mr. Milwaukee's going to follow us?"

"I had to agree to share the story with him to get the information we wanted, and knowing Johnny, he's going to pull the carpet from underneath me and take the scoop to Mr. August himself."

"You don't trust the guy, do you?"

"No, I don't. Which is a shame, but it's the nature of the beast."

Haley and Samantha drove to South Boston were many Irish immigrants had settled. Haley eased to a stop in front of an apartment then stared at her notes. "The first address I have is here, on the first floor."

They were greeted by a little white-haired old lady who had trouble hearing.

"Are you Mrs. Keating?"

"Huh?"

"Mrs. Keating?"

The woman shook her head. "No-no-no."

For a moment, Haley felt confused. Had she gotten the address wrong?

"My daughter is Mrs. Keating." The lady had a definite Irish lilt. "I'm Mrs. Joyce."

"Oh, is Mrs. Keating home?" Haley asked.

"Huh?"

Haley raised her voice. "Is your daughter home?"

"She's not home. She's shopping."

Haley gave Samantha a look of defeat. They weren't going to get far with Mrs. Joyce.

"We'll come back later," Haley said.

"Huh?"

Haley worried she'd have the neighbors pouring into the hallway if she spoke any louder, but the arrival of a frazzled dark-haired woman rescued her.

Samantha opened the door. "Let me help you." She eased a bag out of one arm, and Haley did the same with the other.

"Thank you," the lady said. "It's my brother's birthday, and in my family, birthdays involve big celebrations. I feel like I live at the grocery mart."

"Are you Mrs. Keating?"

"I am." She nodded with her head for them to follow her inside the apartment. "It's okay, Mam," she said loudly. "Friends!"

She looked at Haley and Samantha apologetically. "It's just easier than explaining." She set her bags on the kitchen counter, and Haley and Samantha did the same.

The apartment was surprisingly spacious and well cared for.

Mrs. Keating faced them. "What can I do for you?"

"Are you related to someone called Sean?" Samantha asked.

"I'm Irish," she answered with a smile. "We're all related to someone called Sean."

Samantha clarified. "Sean Keating."

"Sean's my son."

Haley and Samantha shared a look. Mrs. Keating looked too young to be the mother of the man in the photograph. "How old is he?"

"He's twelve. Why?"

"We're looking for a family with an older Sean," Samantha said, showing the photograph. "And someone who looks like him."

Mrs. Keating furrowed full, dark brows. "Who are you again?"

"Please pardon our manners," Haley said. "I'm Dr. Higgins, assistant chief pathologist, and this is Miss Hawke with the *Boston Daily Record*."

Mrs. Keating's good nature darkened. "Sounds serious. But I'm afraid I can't help you. Now, unless you'd like to stay for the party, I really have to start cooking."

"Nice lady," Samantha said as they headed back to the car. "My gut tells me she's telling the truth."

"Mine too," Haley said. "Maybe we'll have better luck at the next one."

The next three calls were equally futile, which made Haley a little nervous because the next one was sure to be uncomfortable. Driving back to the North End, she parked on Stillman.

Samantha stiffened. "What are we doing here?"

"This is the final address."

And the tenement building Samantha lived in.

"Are you aware of any Keatings in the building?" Haley asked gently.

Samantha swallowed. "Families are moving in and

out all the time. I haven't been keeping track." She sighed. "Bina would know. She's very distrusting of anyone who's not Jewish and watches who's who and where like an army general."

"Or, maybe the directory by the door has been updated," Haley said. They walked together to the front door and stared at the list of names.

"I never pay attention to this, but maybe I should." Samantha pointed to a new entry. "Keating."

The Keating family lived at the end of the hall on the third floor. The musky smells of cigarette smoke and fried fish dinners lingered. Haley caught a glimpse of Samantha swallowing back her embarrassment.

A radio played in the background on the other side of the door. Samantha knocked loudly, and an older man in a white shirt and suspenders answered the door.

"Whatever you're selling, I'm not buying." He started to close the door but Samantha put her foot in the way. "I'm a tenant in the building too," she said with a smile. "Second floor. I'm just wondering if you know of a man called Sean Keating?"

"Alive or dead?"

Haley answered, "Dead, sir."

"Died last year?"

Haley nodded.

"Second cousin. Dark horse. That's all I can really say. What's this about?"

"Did your cousin have a brother or another cousin who resembled him?" Samantha asked.

"Everyone in the family says he and Cormac could be twins."

Haley lifted her chin. "Where's Cormac now?"

"I have no idea."

THE FIRST THING Samantha did when she got back to her desk was to call the police station and ask for Officer Bell.

"Hey, Samantha," he answered cheerily. "What can I do for you?"

"Hi, Tom. I'm after a bit of information. Do you think you could meet me?" If Samantha wanted honesty from Tom about the possibility of unethical cops, she couldn't expect him to talk to her with other officers listening.

"I'm on duty right now—"

"It's about the John Doe found at St. Stephen's Church. I might have information."

"Oh, all right. How about Café Vittoria on Hanover."

Samantha appreciated that Tom chose a place within walking distance for her. The late summer heat could still be oppressive, and she already felt wilted. After she hung up with Tom Bell, she spent some time in the restroom freshening up. She told herself it was only to stay professional looking, and not about Tom Bell and his interest in her.

The coffee shop had the advantage of being on a corner, giving it a light and friendly atmosphere. Round tables dotted the wooden floor with matching round-back wooden chairs with padded floral seat cushions circling them.

Tom was there, seated at one, and had ordered her a cup of coffee and a piece of apple pie. "It's on me," he said when she was about to protest. "Don't make a fella eat alone."

Samantha settled into a chair opposite Tom. "Thanks."

He smiled back appreciatively. "You're looking good, Samantha. The job treating you well?"

"Yes, fairly. I'm thankful to have a job. Any day now, I expect a guy to elbow me out, complaining that I'm stealing work from a man who needs it more."

A look of indignation flashed behind Tom's eyes. "You're not getting hounded by that Milwaukee fella, are ya? Because, if he crosses a line—" He smacked his palm with a fist. "Just let me know."

"Tom!"

He cracked a smile. "I mean it in the most legal of ways."

"Well, it's not necessary. I know how to manage Mr. Milwaukee."

Her protestation didn't bring a look of comfort to her officer friend. Samantha took a bite of pie to change the subject. "Oh, this is good."

Tom Bell relaxed his position and dug into his own pie. He followed up with a long sip of his coffee. "What's the information that you have on the John Doe case?"

"I have a name. Cormac Keating."

Tom swallowed hard. "How did you find that out?"

Find that out? He knew.

Samantha's nerves tingled. Could Tom Bell be *dirty?* He was too nice. Too attentive.

Too nice. *Too* attentive. Exactly what a smart dirty cop would be.

"Samantha?"

Samantha blinked and went on the offensive. "Did you already know?"

"I can't talk about an ongoing case."

Malarkey! Tom talked to her about open cases all the time. He was her contact at the station. "You can't or you won't?"

"Samantha—"

Samantha pushed her unfinished pie to the side,

her appetite destroyed by the possibility of this new revelation.

Tom stared back with intensity. "Where did you get that name?"

Samantha put on her gloves, hoping it signaled the end of their little chat. "I can't give away my sources, Officer Bell. Now, if you'll excuse me. I have a family to get back to."

Samantha grabbed her purse and headed for the door, her mind swirling. If Tom Bell was dirty, then every cop on the force could be too. Her equilibrium faltered. Who, besides Haley, could she trust?

Tom Bell grabbed her elbow on the stoop outside. She stared at his hold on her and then shot him a withering look. He released his grip.

"I'm sorry. Samantha, please. I can't tell you everything I know all the time. Just, this is dangerous. *Really* dangerous. Drop this story."

"And if I don't?"

"I can't promise I can protect you."

Samantha snorted as she walked away. She didn't need protection. She needed answers.

And if Tom Bell thought he would ever get another date with her, well, he could just forget about it!

9

It was a divide and conquer approach: Samantha was to meet with Officer Bell while Haley intruded on Detective Cluney's day.

The detective greeted her gruffly. "Dr. Higgins? Is there another body I don't know about?"

Detective Cluney was a family man, and the photo of his wife and kids balanced precariously near the edge of a cluttered desk. An ashtray overflowed with ash and cigar ends, while a well-used porcelain mug with several coffee-stained rings sat empty nearby. Haley waited for Detective Cluney to offer her a chair, but when he didn't, she remained standing but undaunted.

"Detective Cluney, does the name Cormac Keating mean anything to you?"

The detective scowled in return. "Leave police business to the police, Dr. Higgins. I beg of you."

"I take it that's a yes. Shall I change the name on the corpse's toe tag?"

Detective Cluney sighed heavily. "Sit down, Dr. Higgins."

Finally, Haley thought, the truth?

"How did you figure it out?" Detective Cluney asked, then flapped a thick palm. "Forget it. I don't want to know. Yes, your John Doe is Cormac Keating."

"His brother was killed last year?"

"Uh-huh."

"Why has the department not informed the press? Surely this is newsworthy?"

"Because the issue is bigger than one dead guy, Doctor."

"Underground fight club rings? Illegal gambling?"

Detective Cluney opened a small pine box on his desk and removed a cigar. "You're in the wrong profession, Dr. Higgins. You should join the force." He snapped off the tip with cigar clippers. The procedure made Haley squirm. She'd seen her share of bodies with missing fingers show up in the morgue—the unfortunate victims of ruthless loan sharks who made use of the same sharp device.

Detective Cluney lit the cigar and blew out a stream of sharp but pleasant-smelling smoke. His eyes flashed with indecision as he studied Haley. Whatever debate he was having with himself, Haley hoped he'd side with confiding in her. Finally, with his cigar dangling out of the side of thick lips, the detective pushed out of his chair, lumbered to the office door, and closed it. Back at his desk, he rested the cigar on the ashtray, wove sausage-like fingers together, and leaned in.

"Dr. Higgins, I need your word you'll keep what I tell you next to yourself."

"Of course."

"We got ourselves a problem here at North End station. Bigger than the dead guy at the church."

"Unethical behavior among your men?"

Detective Cluney laughed out loud. "That's one way to put it. I just call them crooked."

"How do you know? Is this why you're not revealing the name of the victim to the press."

"It's been going on for some time, over a year. Came to my attention that something was amiss last year when Sean Keating was killed. Someone on the force went to a lot of trouble to muddy the evidence. Every time we think we're about to close in and raid a fight, we show up and there's nothing. No evidence a fight was ever held or plans for one to be held. Someone is always one step ahead of the force."

"And you don't know who," Haley said.

Detective Cluney grunted. "If I did, we wouldn't be having this conversation."

"Why are you telling me?" Haley had watched the detective wrestle with himself—it hadn't been an easy decision for him to make.

"Because I need your help."

"Oh?"

"Look, I know you have a nose for this kind of thing. You're getting it into my business all the time. But I can't trust my men, not until I catch the dirty one."

"Or ones."

"Or ones." The detective dug the stub of his cigar out of the tray and relit it. "As much as it pains me to say, you're the only one I can trust one hundred percent."

Haley blinked at the backhanded compliment.

"Okay. What do you want me to do?"

"That's just it. I have no idea. And I have no right to ask for your assistance. Quite honestly, this is a dangerous business. You saw the body of Keating. Nasty."

"Yes," Haley said carefully. "It reminded me of Joe."

Detective Cluney stared back. "I guessed you'd figure that. Which is why I decided to let you in on company secrets. You'll investigate it, no matter what I say."

Haley smirked. "Yes, Detective. I will."

SAMANTHA HAD a strange feeling she was being followed. It was a sensation she'd felt for the last few days, and she blamed it on a lack of sleep or the stress of her job. Investigative reporting had proved to be a hazardous business, and it was normal she'd be more on edge now than she used to be, right?

Maybe she was paranoid, but she picked up her steps on her way home from work anyway. The roads and alleys grew slimmer as she got closer to the tenements, which cast eerie shadows.

She turned the corner onto Stillman Street where she was jerked into an alley. A dirty palm pressed over her mouth, and fear paralyzed her. Struggling didn't free her, and her whimpers grew desperate sounding as she breathed hard through her nose. Her heart hammered in her chest, and for a moment, she thought she would pass out.

"Hey, baby," a male voice said.

Samantha froze. Good golly. She knew that voice.

She stilled, and the man turned her until she saw his face. If she *had* been the fainting type, she would've dropped to the ground. Seth Rosenbaum, her no-good husband who'd deserted her and Talia, stood in front of her as real as rain. His too-long hair stuck out of a flat cap, and bristles covered his stupid grin.

"Happy to see me?"

Samantha's jaw dropped. Seth had come back to life.

"Say somethin', sugar."

"I thought you were dead."

"Yeah, sorry about that. Necessary evil. Had to stay away until I got some things worked out."

"*Seven* years?"

"Yeah, but it's all good now. I'm home."

Samantha tried to identify the emotions swirling through her soul. Disbelief, anger . . . fear.

"I-I don't know what to say."

Seth frowned, deep and hard. "You can say that you missed me, and you're glad that I'm back."

The thing was Samantha hadn't missed Seth, at least not this version of the man she'd met and married so long ago. Their romance had been more about desire than love, and the unplanned baby that resulted was what had led them to the altar. What she felt now was as far from glad as you could get, but something in his eyes cautioned her from admitting it.

"Of course I missed you. I'm glad you're back. I'm just in shock. It's been so long, Seth."

"Like I said, couldn't be helped. He took her arm. "Let's go."

"Go where?"

"Home. Where else?"

Samantha's mind scrambled. "Have you been there already?" Had Seth been to see his mother before he saw his wife? Her blood cooled at the next thought— had he seen Talia?

"Nah. I wanted to see you first. You look amazing, sugarplum. Too good to be walking the streets unchaperoned."

Stunned, Samantha walked with Seth to their tenement building. She felt slapped—no trampled. Just like the day when Seth had failed to come home, she felt the axis of her world tilt. Seth Rosenbaum was back, and life would never be the same.

10

-----

*H*aley felt as if she'd been given an honorary place on the force, alongside the other women who served there—like Acting Sergeant Margaret McHugh.

But now that she'd been given free rein, she was stumped as to where to begin. All her files on Joe's murder were at her home office, so she turned her DeSoto around and headed to her apartment. The leaves of the elm trees along the sidewalks blew gently in the wind, the breeze faintly saline from the harbor.

Inside her building, the smell of fresh baking filled the hallways—Molly wasn't the only skilled cook and baker on the premises—and Haley's stomach reminded her that it'd been a couple of hours since lunch with Samantha.

She and Molly rarely locked the apartment during

the day, and Haley simply turned the knob and stepped inside.

"Molly, it's me."

"Oh, I have to go," Molly said, but not in response to Haley's announcement. It sounded as if she was talking on the telephone. "Dr. Higgins is here. Why? I don't know. You'll have to ask her yourself. Okay, yes, goodbye for now."

Haley removed her hat and gloves and set them on the side table. She examined the rare Higgins family photo hanging framed on the wall. They'd gathered outside on the front steps of their house on the farm, her parents in the middle with Ben and Harley-James on one side and Joe and Haley on the other. Haley smiled at the fond memories of her childhood, when she'd cared for chickens, milked cows, and played kick the can and rudimentary baseball with her brothers.

Her parents were gone, along with Joe. Ben and his wife and new baby lived on the farm now. Harley-James had gone west to seek his fortune.

"Who was that on the phone?" Haley asked, though she had a good inkling she knew who. Molly's flushed cheeks confirmed her suspicions. She smiled and answered her own question, "Dr. Guthrie, perhaps?"

"Oh, you just mind your own business, smarty-pants." Molly busied herself around the kitchen.

Haley opened the Frigidaire and picked up the bottle of milk. Before she'd finished pouring herself a glass, Mr. Midnight hobble-bounced on his three legs to his bowl.

"Speaking of a smarty-pants," Haley said.

Mr. Midnight stared up at her with his piercing yellow eyes, his black pointy ears twitching in anticipation. Haley poured him milk.

"He knows the sound of the Frigidaire opening," Molly said as if she'd taught him the trick. "You'd think I never feed him."

"I think he's getting fat," Haley said. She petted the feline and squeezed his underbelly. "How can we expect him to chase mice if he's never hungry."

Molly protested. "Oh, posh. The poor thing's only got three legs. Let the other four-legged neighborhood cats do the dirty work."

Haley laughed. Had Molly ever had children, they'd all have been spoiled rotten.

"You're home early," Molly stated.

Molly was on of Haley's few confidants, and she relayed her meeting with Detective Cluney. "It's the greenest light I've ever gotten from him."

"That's quite something," Molly agreed. "What are you going to do now?"

"I'm not sure. It's what I've got to figure out."

"Oh, not that I want to get between you and your boss, but Dr. Guthrie wondered where you were."

"Right. I suppose I'd better check in."

Haley dialed the morgue and spoke to Mr. Martin, who reassured her he had everything under control. No autopsies were scheduled for that afternoon, and Dr. Guthrie was reading in his office. By the way her intern emphasized *reading*, she knew he'd fallen asleep at his desk.

Haley took her glass of milk to her office, went to her desk, and removed Joe's file and a pad of paper from the drawer. Wanting a clean page, she ripped off the top sheet. After grabbing a pen, she poised her hand above the paper. What did she know so far? She found it helped her mind to organize the information if she could see it written out.

Similarities between the deaths of Cormac Keating and Joseph Higgins:

- Death by knife wound in the neck.
- Bodies dumped, fists tucked underneath.
- Bruising, old and new, especially fists, face, and abdomen.

What she and Samantha had learned so far:

- Mr. Mulryan, the secretary at St. Stephen's, has a gambling problem.
- Overheard him being threatened by Mr. Delaney, whom Johnny Milwaukee says organizes underground fight clubs.
- Cormac Keating's brother Sean killed last year. Connection?
- Detective Cluney believes there's a crooked cop on the force, perhaps tainting the evidence needed to crack down on the illegal fighting and gambling ring.

Haley realized that she hadn't heard from Samantha about her meeting with Officer Bell. Mr. Martin would've mentioned if she'd called there. Haley returned to the kitchen, which was now empty. A quick glance into the living room revealed that Molly and Mr. Midnight were having an afternoon snooze together on the plush settee. Haley picked up the receiver to the telephone that hung on the kitchen wall. Dialing the *Boston Daily Record*, Haley quietly asked to speak to Miss Hawke.

"I'm sorry, Miss Hawke isn't in at the moment," the cheery receptionist said. "Can I take a message?"

"This is Dr. Higgins."

"Oh, hi, Dr. Higgins. Miss Hawke never came back

after lunch. Between you, me, and the fence post, you're not the only one looking for her."

Haley hung up concerned. Samantha wasn't the type to go AWOL. It could be she was still out with Officer Bell—the two did have a complicated relationship. At any rate, Samantha was a big girl and could take care of herself.

Which brought Haley back to what she should do next.

"Will Delaney," she muttered aloud. Now, how to find him. Haley's first try was the Boston telephone directory, assuming Mr. Delaney owned a telephone. And if she were to call, what would she say? Are you the Will Delaney who runs illegal fight clubs in the city? Even if she landed on the right one, he would hardly admit to that.

Her only conclusion was to visit Mr. Mulryan, who was at best reluctant and uncooperative and at worst, too terrified to talk. But Haley couldn't sit around doing nothing, especially since she had top-brass approval to interfere.

It was getting near to suppertime, and Haley thought she might have better luck with the church secretary if she caught him at home. No excuses about getting back to church work. She'd found his home address in the church directory she'd picked up when she and Samantha had attended mass.

When Mr. Mulryan opened the door of his cellar apartment beneath a brownstone townhouse, he couldn't contain his shock at seeing Haley step in front of him. He stepped out as if to block her from seeing inside, or rather, to prevent the missus from seeing her.

"What are you doing here?"

"I was hoping you'd give me a minute of your time, Mr. Mulryan. I'm looking for someone who attends your parish, and he's not in your directory. I thought maybe you would know where he lives."

"Very well," Mr. Mulryan said impatiently. "Who is it?"

"Will Delaney."

Mr. Mulryan swallowed hard. "What do you need with the likes of him?"

"I'm investigating the death of my brother." Haley thought it best not to bring up the body in the church-yard. "I have reason to believe they might've known each other."

"Take my advice, Dr. Higgins, and walk away."

"Do you know where Mr. Delaney resides?"

Mr. Mulryan stepped forward. "Dr. Higgins, do you want to end up like your brother?"

He knew her brother? "Is that a threat?"

"What? No! These people are dangerous, Doctor. You don't know what they're capable of."

Mr. Mulryan turned and headed inside. Much to his exasperation, Haley stayed on his heels.

"What are you doing?"

"Tell me where I can find Mr. Delaney, or I'm going to introduce myself to your wife and tell her why I'm here."

"Fine, but your blood is on your own hands."

Mr. Mulryan spat a Beacon Hill address then slammed the door in Haley's face.

BEACON HILL WAS A PRESTIGIOUS NEIGHBORHOOD, and it was no surprise when Haley learned Mr. Delaney occupied the penthouse suite of a well-to-do complex along Storrow Drive. She was stopped by the doorman.

"Might I have your name, ma'am?" he asked politely.

"Dr. Haley Higgins. I'm here to see Mr. William Delaney."

"Is he expecting you, ma'am."

Haley hesitated. Then she did something uncharacteristic—she lied. "Yes. I've got something he's requested." She patted her purse as if she carried narcotics or cocaine, something a man like Mr. Delaney might take part in. What *was* in her bag was a Harrington & Richardson nine-shot pistol. It usually rested in her lower desk drawer, locked away, but something had told her it was time to pack it along.

The doorman eyed a telephone on his desk, and Haley could see the deliberation. Apparently, Mr. Delaney did not like to be interrupted. Haley cleared her throat, and when she saw the doorman glance her way, she made a point of looking at her wristwatch.

"I'm rather late. Mr. Delaney's going to be upset with me." She smiled her most pathetic-looking smile. "If you don't mind, I'm going to get into the elevator."

Not waiting for permission, Haley moved quickly, stepped into the elevator, and instructed the attendant.

"Penthouse."

It wasn't the elevator attendant's job to question those who got in. He pressed the button, and the doors closed. Haley let out a long slow breath. Another obstacle conquered.

The elevator lumbered to the top floor and shuddered to a stop. The metal doors fanned opened, and instead of producing a usual type of hallway, Haley found herself inside the home of Mr. Delaney. He stood there as if he'd expected her, a glass of whiskey in hand.

"Dr. Higgins," he said. "Mr. Wiles, my doorman, just called to profusely apologize. Apparently, he was incapable of stopping a most-determined female who professed to have something of interest in her purse for me. I do hope that is true."

"Forgive my ruse, Mr. Delaney," Haley said. "I feared a little white lie was the only way I'd be able to speak to you."

"You have my attention. But, please come in and have a seat. If I'm forced to be hospitable, allow me to do a decent job of it. Can I get you a drink?"

Haley thought him very brazen to make a presentation of the drink in his hand, considering the possession of alcohol remained illegal.

"I'm quite fine," Haley said. "Thank you." She accepted a soft-leather armchair and sat carefully on the edge of it in case she needed to make a defensive move.

The interior walls of the suite were papered with black and white Art Deco geometric lines. An exquisite polished teakwood wall unit had sliding doors perfect for concealing prohibited beverages like the one Mr. Delaney sipped. Tall windows offered a stunning view over the Charles River and into Cambridge.

"Beautiful spot you have here," she said.

Several photographs hung on the wall, including landscapes of Boston city. Her eye was drawn to an image of Long Wharf and the row of warehouses stationed there.

"I like to watch the ships come in," Mr. Delaney said. "Such a busy place, this harbor."

Haley pivoted to face him. "And yet the Depression continues."

"There are rich, and there are poor," Will Delaney said sanguinely. "And so, it will always be." His gaze stayed on her as he sipped from his crystal glass. "Now, you didn't come here to discuss social ills, surely?"

"I'm looking for information," Haley said. "My brother was murdered several years ago, and his case was never solved."

"My sympathies, but I fail to see how I can help."

"I'm not sure if you can either," Haley said. "But I have reason to believe Joe was involved in illegal fight clubs. I've been told you might know something about it."

Mr. Delaney cocked his head. "Really? And how would *I* know?"

Haley shrugged. "I'm not with the police." Not exactly a white lie. "I just want to know what happened to my brother."

"And how will that help you? It won't bring him back from the dead."

"No, I suppose not. How did you make your fortune, Mr. Delaney?" A quick change of subject sometimes unraveled a suspect. Haley didn't think

Will Delaney would be so easily put off guard, and she was right. The man smirked.

"Imports and exports, Dr. Higgins."

Not gambling and organizing underground fight clubs? She didn't pose the question aloud.

Mr. Delaney stood. "I'm sorry that I can't be of more help to you on your personal quest for answers, but I am a very busy man."

Haley took her cue and got to her feet. She didn't know what she'd hoped to discover by such a bold move.

She stretched out her hand, a gesture of goodwill. Will Delaney smirked and accepted her hand, but as he stretched out his arm, the cuff of his sleeve crept up, revealing a tattoo.

Haley pretended not to notice, but the two combat spiders etched on the inside of Mr. Delaney's wrist was hard to miss.

11

————

Samantha panted as she rushed after Seth. "Maybe I should go inside first." Still numb with shock that Seth Rosenbaum, in the flesh, had shown up, she followed him up the dingy steps to their second-floor apartment. It'd been so long, Samantha was surprised that Seth even remembered where they lived!

"Just to prepare Bina," she added. Even though it was only two floors of stairs, Samantha felt short of breath. "She's gotten frail since you've been gone. You wouldn't want her to die from shock, would you?"

Seth stopped on the landing and considered her. "Yeah, okay. Two minutes, huh?"

Samantha didn't waste a second. She felt a responsibility to warn Bina, but most of all, she wanted to know where Talia was, hoping beyond hope this was the day she went to her friend Sarah's place after school. Why didn't she know this? She was such a terrible mother!

Using her key to unlock the door, she stepped in quietly and closed the door behind her.

"Bina?"

The apartment was small, and Samantha knew that Bina had heard her come inside.

"In the kitchen."

Samantha sprinted to her mother-in-law who looked up with wide eyes. "What's the matter with you, sneaking up on me? Why are you home already?" She squinted. "Is something wrong?"

"Where's Talia?"

"She's with her friend Sarah. Why? What's wrong? You look ill."

Samantha pulled out a chair and motioned with her gloved hand. "Maybe you should sit."

Bina, stubborn as ever, gripped the back of the wooden, ladder-back chair. "I will not. Now speak to me."

"It's Seth."

Bina automatically paled. "They found him?"

"No. He's not dead, Bina. He's alive." Samantha stared at the door. "He's in the hallway."

The knob turned as both women stared, and then the door burst open.

"Hi, *Eema*! It's me."

Bina's knees gave out, and she landed on the chair.

"Eema. I'm back."

Seth continued to make his pronouncement as if Samantha and Bina should break out the wine in celebration.

Did he not realize what he'd put them through? Samantha thought.

"Eema?" Seth said with a look of confusion.

Bina found the strength to get to her feet. "My boy. Come to Eema."

Seth's long arms nearly smothered his petite mother. Bina jumped to action. "You must be hungry. I'll make you supper, *kugel,* maybe? And coffee, eh? We don't have any sugar, but it's good black, no?"

And suddenly, it was like Seth had never left. Bina doted, and Seth beamed.

Samantha felt sick, confused, and somehow out of breath. "I have to go," she said.

"What?" Seth said sharply. "I just got home."

"Well, I have a job, and I can't dictate my own hours. I'll see you later. Bye, Bina."

Seth called out, "Babe!" But Samantha moved down the steps like a strong breeze. She pushed the door open and kept walking.

Her mind spun with every clip-tap of her shoes on the sidewalk. Seth was back, but where had he come from? Where'd he been all these years? Maybe, if he showed signs of having suffered from amnesia, she could understand how he could've stayed away so long, but he was the same arrogant, entitled son-of-a-gun he'd been before he disappeared.

When she looked up, she found she was at the *Boston Daily Record* building. Like a horse that always knows the way home, she mused. She hurried inside. The last thing she needed was to get sacked for slacking off.

She stared blankly at the typewriter before rolling in a fresh piece of paper. What story had she even been working on, anyway?

"Hey, doll, you okay? It's late in the day for you around here."

Samantha glanced up at her cocky coworker, but her mind failed her. Instead of a snarky comeback, her eyes, to her horror, watered-up.

In an instant, Johnny was at her desk. He squatted, eye-level, and placed a gentle hand on her shoulder. "What's wrong, Sam?"

Samantha's lips quivered. She felt a torrent building up, and helpless to defy it, she reached for a handkerchief. "It's Seth. He's back."

Stupid tears!

Samantha pressed the handkerchief against her eyes, and when she felt the warmth of Johnny's arms wrap around her, she just let him hold her.

12

———

*H*aley and Molly discussed the case over breakfast the next morning.

"Though the North End of Boston isn't a large landmass," Haley said as she buttered her toast, "there are innumerable warehouses, especially on the docks, that could be used for illegal fighting clubs."

"What do you know so far?" Molly asked.

"I've only a bit of clay as a clue to the location of the one where Cormac Keating died." Haley sighed. She couldn't help but feel a little deflated.

The kettle whistle sounded for tea, and Molly rose to pour the hot water into the teapot. Mr. Midnight made his usual entrance, with a hobble and a meow, having long since learned that the whistle meant tea and thus milk. Molly added milk to the bottom of the teacups before pouring the tea, making a third pour into Mr. Midnight's bowl.

Haley smiled at the white mustache the cat created while vigorously lapping, his long pink tongue darting out to clean away the evidence.

"If I could at least find the scene of the crime," Haley went on, "maybe another clue would present itself. It's all rather frustrating. Someone's going to a lot of effort to clean up. We know two Keating brothers are dead, and who knows how many bodies have ended up in the harbor."

"Has Peter been any help?"

"Peter?"

Molly blinked then glanced away. "Dr. Guthrie."

"Oh."

Molly and Dr. Guthrie were on a first-name basis! How awkward. Haley couldn't imagine ever bringing herself to call her boss by his Christian name, and she couldn't imagine him calling her Haley either.

"It's not a big deal, Dr. Higgins," Molly said. "A slip of the tongue."

Did Molly not notice she still called Haley *Doctor*?

"Uh, no. Beyond examining the body, Dr. Guthrie's not actively involved in this investigation."

Mr. Midnight, having licked his bowl clean, started on his bathing sequence—wetting his paw and swiping at his ear.

Haley checked the time on her watch. "I should go." If she wanted to slip out to do more investigating, she'd better have all her paperwork done before she went. "Thanks for breakfast, Molly."

"Will you be home for dinner?"

An odd question. Haley rarely missed the evening meal. Did Molly want to make other plans?

"I'm not sure."

"I'll leave a casserole in the refrigerator, in case I'm out."

Haley refrained from the grumble that churned within. She had no right to negative feelings, but she didn't like this new relationship between Molly and Dr. Guthrie. Had Haley known that Molly was so inclined, Haley would've tried to set her up, much earlier, with someone who wasn't her boss.

It was a short walk down Grover Street past the county jail and onto the hospital property. Haley, wearing a favorite pair of wide-leg slacks, hurried toward the hospital, and though she'd been sure she'd be the first to arrive, Dr. Guthrie had beaten her there. More surprisingly, he was performing a postmortem.

"Another John Doe?" Haley asked.

"No. Heart attack," Dr. Guthrie grumbled. "The autopsy, requested and paid for by the family, was quite unnecessary, as nothing new has been learned."

Just at that moment, the intern, Mr. Martin,

stepped in. "Oh good," Dr. Guthrie said to him without a greeting. "You can sew him up."

"Certainly, Dr. Guthrie." Mr. Martin had a sheet of paper in his hand. He offered it to Haley. "It's the laboratory results on your piece of dirt."

Haley grabbed the sheet, read the results, and stared up blankly. "Figs?" The report was clear. Dirt from the bottom of someone's boots had trace elements of the exotic fruit. Whoever had dumped Mr. Keating's body at St. Stephen's Churchyard, must work at one of the import docks, or possibly aboard one of the ships.

It was a shot in the dark, but it was still a clue.

Haley knew what she had to do. She made a pot of tea and brought a tray in to Dr. Guthrie. He stared back with his bushy eyebrows raised.

"Dr. Guthrie, I wanted to let you know that I'm doing a little work for Detective Cluney and will be out for most of the morning."

Dr. Guthrie stirred sugar into his tea. "What kind of work? Surely not *police* work."

Haley didn't want to get into how the detective mistrusted his force.

He mumbled further, "They get their own funding for that."

And here Haley thought her boss was concerned for her safety.

LEE STRAUSS

"Consider it an act of goodwill," she said. "One day, we might need their help."

At first, Samantha thought she'd had a bad dream. She awoke to the morning light streaming in through threadbare curtains just before her alarm clock was about to ring. Talia was curled in an angelic ball beside her.

But then the truth tumbled down like a lopsided wall of bricks.

After Samantha had confided in Johnny, he insisted on driving her home in his roadster. Even though he knew she lived in the tenements, she hated having it broadcasted in such a way. Unfortunately, Seth had been standing at the living room windows and saw the whole thing.

The fight didn't boil until after Talia, whom Bina had collected, had fallen asleep, and Bina had done the same. Poor Talia was so confused. The father she'd longed for was a stranger, and her reaction to Seth had been such—she'd hidden behind Samantha's skirt and was unwilling to go to him.

Samantha had tried to explain. "She needs time to get used to you."

Seth had responded by smiling tightly and then pulling out a Mickey from his suit pocket. He eased off the cap and took a long swig, exhaling loudly as the bootlegged whiskey burned his throat.

Bina had offered to put Talia to bed. Samantha wondered if the rose-colored glasses that Bina had worn for her son these last many years had come off. Samantha thought her mother-in-law actually looked frightened.

"Was that your boyfriend?" Seth had said, his eyes flashing with daring.

"He's a coworker."

"You ran into his arms, didn't you?"

"No! Absolutely not." Samantha had felt the blush of shame rise on the back of her neck. She had found comfort in Johnny's arms, but it wasn't like *that*.

Seth had grabbed her arm then, tightly enough to leave bruises. Samantha subconsciously rubbed the tender spot as she remembered the fear. Seth had changed. The anger, bitterness, and jealousy simmered beneath the surface.

"You won't see him again."

"I can't help but see him. We work at the same paper."

"I'm back now. No wife of mine needs to work."

"You've been gone a very long time, Seth Rosenbaum. You're not about to start telling me what to do now. Besides, I've not seen a penny from you. How do you expect us to live?"

He'd raised his palm, and she'd thought he would slap her, but he held his hand midair. Slowly it fell to his side.

"Sugar. This isn't how I imagined our reunion."

"I imagined it at a funeral, lowering you into the ground."

"You'd like that wouldn't you."

Samantha was ashamed of the feelings that confirmed his accusation. She'd never wished Seth dead, but life would be easier now had it been true.

Seth had stormed out, shouting something about her being a whore and having turned his daughter against him.

SAMANTHA SLIPPED OUT from under the thin summer sheet, careful not to wake Talia. It would be time to rouse her for school soon, but Samantha wanted to check on the status of the rest of the apartment first. She quickly removed the plastic curlers from her hair—just in case Seth was up, then headed to the kitchen.

Bina was tiptoeing about, preparing a pot of porridge. Her tentative, elf-like movements told Samantha that Seth likely slept it off on the couch in the living room. A peek proved that she was right. Seth, on his back, one leg hanging off the edge, and his mouth wide open, let out a low rumble snore.

Samantha failed to understand what she'd ever seen in the man, and now, legally, he was her husband, *'til death do us part*. She turned on her heel and exhaled a long sigh.

Bina put a gnarly finger to her lips and whispered hoarsely, "Let him sleep."

Samantha had every intention of leaving the snoring, drooling, sinewy creature good and well alone.

Talia responded to her admonitions for quiet. "Daddy's been working all night," Samantha said as an excuse. She had no idea what Seth had done through the dark hours.

"Is he all right, Mommy?" she asked as Samantha dressed her.

Good question. "Sure, he is. Just tired from working hard."

"Where was he?"

Another good question.

Samantha crouched to Talia's level and smiled as she stroked her daughter's soft hair. What she'd give to prevent heartache from ever reaching this precious child. Samantha choked down fears that her baby's first real emotional pain would come at the hand of her own father.

"It's a very long story, honey, and Daddy hasn't had

a chance to tell it. The main thing is that he's back now. Lucky, huh?"

Talia ducked her chin. "Uh-huh."

"We have to eat our breakfast quietly today, then Bubba will walk you to school."

Samantha's appetite failed her. Late for work now anyway, she spent the time dressing instead. She'd done something she hadn't done in a while with her last paycheck—bought herself a new dress. A form-fitting cotton print, it had a row of buttons down the front and a hem that flounced at her shins. *A necessary expense*, she reasoned. She couldn't wear rags to work, but now, with Seth back...

She let the thought drift.

Despite Seth's allegations regarding Johnny, and Samantha's denial, she took a little extra time with her makeup. She added a wide-brimmed hat, admired the broad white ribbon and red floral enhancement, and slipped on a pair of summer gloves.

Holding her shoes in her hand, she slipped into the kitchen to kiss Talia on the cheek. "Have a good day, honey. I'll see you after school."

Bina stared at her and then the still body on the couch with unblinking bulbous eyes. If it weren't for Talia, Samantha would catch the next train out of town, but she couldn't leave her daughter, and she couldn't hold down a job without someone to care for Talia.

She was stuck.

As easily as she could, Samantha carefully stepped through the living room, praying her stockings wouldn't snag from a splinter on the wooden floor. She opened the door, but no matter how slowly or cautiously, it let out a squeaky whine.

Seth snorted.

Samantha froze.

The blanket had shifted to expose a pale arm. Samantha squinted at the black smudge on the inside of his wrist. A spider tattoo. Not one spider but two?

A second seemed eternal, but Seth's breathing returned to a natural rhythm. Samantha slipped into the lobby, buckled her sandals, and hurried down the steps.

13

*T*he docks along the harbor jutted eastward from Atlantic Avenue. Driving north, the first to come into view was Foster Wharf, followed by Rowes Wharf and India Wharf. The docks grew in size as the shoreline curved northward to where Central Wharf and Wet Dock, and Long Wharf were located.

Haley had driven down many times since buying the DeSoto and passed row upon row of warehouses that blocked the view of the glistening harbor sea. The docks themselves were dedicated to different shipping lines: Eastern Corp Bangor Line, New York Line, Yarmouth Line, Railway Steamship Line, etcetera.

Haley was interested in the Long Wharf that had warehouses dedicated to Quincy Market Cold Storage to the north and United Fruit Co. to the south.

Figs were fruit, and there was a good chance they were imported at this dock. Not only that, Mr. Delaney had a framed photograph of himself, along with several other men, standing in front of warehouse 21 on the Quincy Market side. It seemed like a reasonable place to start.

Parking the DeSoto, Haley exited and peered eastward. The sun glistened off the water, and she propped a pair of round-lensed sunglasses on her short nose. She'd forgotten to put on her hat, but with a gloved hand, she checked her purse for her pistol. A girl couldn't be too careful. She had purposely chosen a pair of slacks, not wanting to attract the attention a slender skirt often got, especially in an area mostly occupied by the opposite sex.

Wind blew off the harbor and caught her curls, and she pushed them behind her ears. Seagulls squawked loudly as they circled the blue sky above. It was a beautiful day, only spoiled by murder. Haley wasn't sure what she hoped to find. Along the docks, men loaded trucks with boxes stamped with import company names. Cranes with heavy loads moved pallets from ship to dock, men yelling directions to the operator to keep from getting squashed.

"Hey, lady!" one of them yelled.

Haley jumped out of the way, just in time. The crane operator could use lessons!

She shouted back. "Watch it!"

A man approached. "Whatcha doin' on the docks, ma'am? No place for women."

"Do you know if figs are imported through the United Fruit Co.?"

The man's brow collapsed. "Huh?"

"I'm wondering if a shipment of figs came in recently."

"Ya got me. I dunno what's in the boxes half the time. I just do my job and load them on the backs of the trucks. Now, you'd get out of the way if you know what's good for ya."

SAMANTHA FELT as if she'd been walking on rough gravel, with the earth shifting underneath, and vertigo ever threatening. She didn't know how she'd made it to the *Boston Daily Record*, but her legs felt weak as she climbed the stairs. She smiled delicately at the receptionist who greeted her with a cheery, "Good morning!"

The bull pit was busy and loud, a perfect storm of creativity, cussing, smoking, and loud voices. This was the world Samantha knew now, and all at once, she found her sea legs. She removed her hat and gloves, tucked her messenger bag beside her desk, and checked on her camera in the drawer. The typewriter, nude without a sheet of paper bold and waiting, beckoned her. Work would be her saving grace.

Her thoughts went to Tom Bell. She wasn't sure if she could trust him. She hated that she felt unsure. Tom was clean. He was one of the good cops, right?

Right?

"Hey, doll."

Samantha could lie to herself and say she hadn't even noticed Johnny Milwaukee chatting with Fred Hall about the latest sports statistic, shouting instructions to Max, or lighting up a cigarette, but she had registered every slightest movement.

"Hi, Johnny." Her fight had left her, and he noticed. His debonair grin flipped into a frown. He pushed up from his chair and sauntered over.

"How are things, Sam? At home?"

It was such a personal question. Touching yet intrusive. She couldn't confide in another man about her husband, her conflicting feelings about his return, her honest, unchristian thoughts.

"They're fine, Johnny." She forced a smile. "It's a change, but a good one."

Big fat liar, was she!

And she hadn't fooled Johnny.

"I see," was all he said before he stepped backward and returned to his desk. His eyes darted her way once before he threw himself entirely into whatever story he was covering.

She sighed and tried to focus.

Shape your eyebrows like the Hollywood starlets do.

Seth would get a job. She could stay home with Talia. She'd love that.

His return wouldn't be all bad.

But how long would he agree to sleep on the couch? Even though he was her husband, Samantha realized she didn't love him anymore.

What was she going to do?

She startled at the sound of her telephone ringing.

"Front desk," the happy receptionist sang. "Dr. Higgins is in the lobby asking for you."

Samantha grabbed her hat and gloves and put them on.

Johnny's eyebrows jumped. "Big lead?"

"Just lunch with a friend."

Johnny checked his watch. "Kinda early for lunch."

Samantha shrugged. "It's her schedule."

Out of habit, she collected her messenger bag, which contained her notepad and a spare, plenty of sharp pencils, along with female essentials like lipstick and a hairbrush.

She smiled when she saw Haley's friendly face and noted the doctor looked sharp in her cotton slacks, which had a high waist and wide legs, a recent fashion favorite of hers, and briefly pondered if she would one day wear the same. Not likely. For one thing, she'd never be able to afford to follow the trends when they were trending. Her sewing machine was her trick pony, and she'd been able to make old dresses new again with trims, tucks, and add-ons.

"Hello, Haley," she said. "This is a surprise."

"I was in the neighborhood, at the docks, actually," Haley said. "I thought maybe it was time to exchange notes."

"I couldn't agree more."

Samantha was eager to talk about the Keating case, and she had yet to tell Haley about Seth.

Instead of walking to the nearest coffee shop, Haley walked to her car and instructed Samantha to get in.

"Where are we going?" Samantha asked.

"To the docks. I have something to show you."

14

*H*aley immediately sensed that something had happened. She held the car keys in her hand, waited until they were both seated with the doors closed, and stared Samantha in the eye. "What's wrong?"

Samantha swallowed, her eyes relaying a fragility Haley hadn't seen in her friend before.

"Seth's back."

"*What?*"

"He's not dead." Samantha's gaze veered blankly out the car window. "He's very, very alive."

"Good golly." This news had so many implications. "Where was he all this time?"

"I don't know. We haven't had a chance to get into it. We've already had a big fight."

"About what?" It was an impertinent question, but it rolled out before Haley could stop it.

"Johnny."

"Johnny? How absurd."

"I fell apart at the office and Johnny . . . uh . . . well . . . he drove me home."

Those hesitations spoke louder than words, but Haley had to be careful not to cross a line. She was already dangerously close to traipsing into areas that weren't any of her business.

Samantha continued, "Seth saw me get out of Johnny's roadster." She blinked back tears. "It's just all so crazy. I thought he was dead. It's like a ghost came back to life. Oh, Haley, I don't know what's going to happen now. I don't know my place anymore."

"Your place is right here with me," Haley said. "At least for today." She started the ignition, then glanced at Samantha with an admonishing grin. "Let's solve this case, shall we?"

Haley headed for State Street then east toward the harbor.

"What's at the docks?" Samantha asked. "Did you find something?"

"I'm not sure. I need a second opinion." Haley glanced at her passenger, satisfied to see a pleased look at her suggestion that Samantha was needed. She brought Samantha up to date with her meeting with Will Delaney and the trace of fig in the clay.

"Fig? How peculiar," Samantha said. "But going to see Mr. Delaney alone? Next time, you must take me with you."

Haley was delighted with Samantha's use of the words "next time". Hopefully, with the sudden addition of Seth Rosenbaum to the equation, some things wouldn't change too dearly.

"What about you?" Haley asked as she searched for a place to park. "Learn anything interesting from Officer Bell."

"You know, I don't know. I hate to say this, but I think he might be a dirty cop."

Haley had just pulled into a space behind a grocery delivery truck. She turned her head sharply. "Why do you say that?"

"He was very evasive when I tried to talk to him."

"That's just a cop thing."

"But he's usually quite open with me about his work. We have an—understanding."

"Still, there could be a lot of reasons why he was stingy with information this time. Though Detective Cluney suspects he has at least one crooked officer on the force, which is how he explains the loss of evidence, his inability to clamp down on these fight clubs, and his failure to solve the Keating brothers murders."

"Drat," Samantha said with a huff. "I was hoping I was mistaken."

"It doesn't mean that Officer Bell is the guilty party."

A gray mass of clouds billowed in from the horizon, and droplets fell at their feet. Samantha produced an umbrella from her messenger bag. "Do you want to share?"

"That's all right." Haley said, "I have one under my seat. Bring your camera."

They huddled under Haley's black and Samantha's yellow and blue umbrellas as Haley led the way. "The rain is bad," she said soberly. "It'll wash away evidence."

They strolled on the boardwalk past Quincy Market Cold Storage and Warehouse Co. and United Fruit Co.

"It's in here."

The small alley was sheltered, thankfully, by the overhanging roofs of both structures. Haley pointed to reddish-brown splatters on the wooden siding.

"Blood," she said. "I've already taken samples for the lab. Blood typing might help us to confirm if this belongs to Cormac Keating."

Samantha had her camera out and snapped. "This is the scene of the crime?"

"I believe so," Haley said. "And look at this."

Haley directed Samantha's attention to a discarded wooden box, splintered in the middle as if it had been stepped on.

"What is it?" Samantha said.

"Take your photographs first."

As Samantha removed her black Kodak box camera from its case, Haley produced a paper evidence bag and picked up the crushed box with her gloved hand. On the top were the faded words painted in green, Mediterranean Figs.

"My theory," Haley started, "is that the killer stepped on this box and a remnant of its former contents got caught up in the body or on the bottom of his boot, as he carried it away."

Before Samantha could respond, they were interrupted by a male voice. "Hey!"

Haley and Samantha stilled. They both knew the voice.

"Officer Bell?" Haley said.

Tom Bell wore his official blue police uniform, the brass buttons on his double-breasted jacket done up to the chin, a flat cap with a black bill on his head. His lips worked as he processed the two ladies in front of him.

"What are you doing here? You're trespassing on private property."

Samantha jutted her chin up in defiance. "I'm following a lead on a story."

"Well, you can't be here." His gaze moved to Haley, beseeching. "Dr. Higgins, I have to ask you to leave."

"We've got everything we wanted," Haley said.

Officer Bell's frown deepened. "I'm not supposed to let you take evidence."

"Oh, it's quite all right," Haley said. "Detective Cluney gave me the go-ahead. You can ask him yourself."

It was clear that Tom Bell was in a pickle. Haley was reasonably certain that his instructions hadn't come from the police. If that were the case, then who was Officer Bell taking his instructions from?

Samantha quickly put her camera back in its bag when they were joined by two other policemen. She recognized them from the policeman's ball, Officers Harris and McAteer.

"What's this, Bell?" Officer McAteer said.

Officer Bell replied, "These ladies were just leaving."

Officer Harris glared at them, his eyes darting to the stain on the wall and back. "Are you lost?"

"Uh, ya know," Samantha said sheepishly. "I felt ill

and thought a bit of ocean air would settle my stomach. We darted in this alley so I could . . ." She made a hard swallow motion as if she were about to vomit.

"This is no place for women," Officer McAteer said. He stared back at Tom Bell. "Officer Bell, please escort them back to their vehicle."

15

"I need to ask you for your film." Tom Bell looked very unhappy as he reached out a hand to Samantha. She jerked back.

"I don't think so."

"Samantha."

"Officer Bell," Samantha returned. No more first names for him. "I know my rights, and as a private citizen, I can take all the personal photos I like."

"But—"

"Unless you can prove a crime has been committed, which I know you can't, then you must let us go on our way unmolested."

Samantha couldn't believe the nerve of the man. And drat it all! She'd have to find a new contact on the force, and that wasn't an easy task.

Thankfully, Haley had dug her heels in as well.

"Miss Hawke has made several good points. I do hope you have a good reason for trying to detain us."

"I have a damn good reason! I'm trying to protect you."

Haley, with a calmness Samantha envied, said, "From whom, Officer Bell?"

Tom Bell's shoulders fell. "I can't say, but knowing you two, you've probably put a few bits together. Now, don't be sore, but I can't be seen chatting it up with you. Just leave things alone for once!"

"Why?" Samantha demanded. She was furious. She had trusted Tom, but now he wouldn't trust her. And here she'd practically saved his life once. "You know what, I don't care if I never see you again. You men are alike. Users, takers, liars!" She spun on her heel on the wet dock nearly losing her balance, saved from a surely ungraceful fall by Tom Bell himself. She tugged her arm from his grasp, stomped to the DeSoto, and got in the passenger side without looking back.

Tom stared open-mouthed.

"She's going through a lot right now," Samantha heard Haley say. Haley left Tom Bell to figure out women and the plight of mankind and joined Samantha in the car. The windshield had fogged up.

Haley wiped the inside of the windshield with her handkerchief. "You're breathing too hard."

"I just made a fool of myself, didn't I?"

"We all have our bad days."

"Do you?" Samantha challenged. "You always seem so cool and collected. So intelligent and intuitive."

"I've misstepped in the past, believe me."

"With Officer Thompson?"

Haley stomped on the brake. It was a coincidence, Samantha noted, as she watched a black-topped Ford cut them off.

Haley honked the horn, and she shifted down a gear before saying, "What do you mean?"

"I see how he looks at you. And you're not that great at hiding the fact that you look back at him."

"We had something once."

"Let me guess," Samantha said. "You got scared and ended it."

"I did *not* get scared."

This time an aggressive bout of honking came from a passing vehicle, its driver giving Haley a stern look. Samantha could tell she'd hit a nerve because Haley was normally a very astute driver.

"But you did end it."

"We met shortly after Joe died. The only thing I cared about at that time? Solving his murder. Besides, Jack was leaving town to work in the Midwest for a stint."

"And now?"

"And now what?"

"Do you care about more than one thing? Do you care about him?"

"Samantha! Your personal crisis has made you overly bold."

Samantha felt properly chastised. Seth did this to her. Made her feel defensive and unsteady. "I'm sorry, Haley. I'm not in my right mind. Please forgive me."

Haley pulled to a stop in front of the *Boston Daily Record* building "It's fine. I know you have a lot on your mind."

Samantha grabbed her things. Had she just sabotaged the one relationship, besides what she had with her daughter, that meant anything to her? "Thanks for bringing me along," she said. "I'll let you know when I get the photographs developed."

She was about to get out of the car when Haley said, "Samantha?"

"Yes."

Haley reached out her gloved hand, and Samantha took it. "I'm sorry for snapping at you. I'll tell you the story one day."

Samantha smiled back. "Only if you want to."

HALEY WASN'T sure if she'd ever want to or not, but decided to turn the focus back to Samantha. "You were rather hard on Officer Bell back there."

Samantha sniffed. "What if he's the dirty cop?"

"What if he's not?"

"You're right." Staring out the window, Samantha released a long, slow breath. "I'm just not myself today."

Haley sympathized. Seth Rosenbaum's return had rocked the boat. The question only time would tell was just how wet was everyone going to get? She changed the subject. "Officer Harris rubs me the wrong way."

"Do you think he's our bad cop?"

"Who's to say? I do wonder what Officer McAteer and Officer Bell were up to. I have a hard time believing they were on a randomly scheduled foot beat."

"They're protecting someone," Samantha said.

"Or investigating," Haley countered. "They might've ended up there following the same clues we did."

"Dr. Higgins, you're so sensible."

Sarcastic or sincere, Haley couldn't tell, and quite honestly, she didn't want to know.

Samantha reached for the door handle, then froze, inhaling sharply.

"What's the matter?" Haley asked. Then she followed Samantha's gaze to a man leaning against the red-brick wall of the newspaper building. His right knee was bent with the foot of his worn leather shoe pressed against the bricks, a straw boater covered his eyes, while a lit cigarette hung from the corner of his mouth. Haley had never met Seth Rosenbaum before, had never seen a picture, but she knew without a doubt it was he who glared in Samantha's direction.

"He's changed," Samantha said. "He was always a scoundrel, but I'd never been . . ." Samantha stopped and stared at her hands.

Haley finished for her. "Afraid?"

Samantha didn't answer. She pulled the handle, pushed the door open, and stepped out.

"Do you want me to come with you?" Haley asked.

Samantha shook her head. "It's not necessary."

Haley didn't drive off immediately, even though staying was obviously an intrusive effort to spy on a personal moment. She didn't trust Mr. Rosenbaum and worried about Samantha's safety. She would wait until Samantha went inside.

Haley couldn't hear what they said to each other, but from the look on Seth's sour face, he wasn't happy to see his wife. Samantha appeared to stand up to him, and Haley silently cheered her on. When Seth grabbed Samantha's arm, Haley pulled on her door handle. She didn't know what she would do to break it up between them—make a scene, press on her car horn?

Her hand rested on the side of her purse, on the outline of her gun.

But none of the options that flew through her mind in that split second were necessary. Samantha jerked out of Seth's grip and ran inside. Seth, wisely, didn't follow her.

Haley sighed. She felt deep sorrow for her friend. If she'd thought her life was hard while Seth had been missing, it was most definitely going to get worse now that he had been found.

THE NERVE OF THAT MAN! Samantha thought. *Demanding I should quit my job! On the spot just like that?*

Ignoring the cheery receptionist, Samantha fumed as she took quick strides straight to her desk. She sat in a huff, not removing her hat or gloves, just letting her messenger bag and camera case thud to the floor by her feet. Her eyes blurred as she stared at the typewriter, the last sheet of paper she'd rolled into it still waiting.

What was she going to do? Seth had all the rights, all the leverage, and apparently, a good amount of money. At least that was what he claimed. Samantha didn't even want to know where that money had come from; it most certainly hadn't been acquired legally.

Seth claimed he had a job, but he wouldn't say

what, only that she was to trust him.

"Remember our vows, baby. You have to obey me."

Samantha huffed.

She'd fight him on that—she would've fought him on that—if it weren't for what he said next. He'd take Talia and Bina and leave Boston without her.

Samantha couldn't help herself. She lifted her gloved hands to her face and cried.

"See?" Fred Hall howled from the other side of the pit. "This is why I say no women in the pit. She's crying. This job is meant for men. A reporter needs backbone. You never know what you're going to see or what you'll have to do."

"Shut up!" Samantha glared at the sports man through her tears. "I've seen more blood and gore and have been in more danger working at this paper in the last six months than you've seen in sixteen years! Nose bleeds on the ball field don't count as gore!"

Johnny, who Samantha only now noticed, slowly clapped.

"Just admit it that you love the dame," Fred said, sneering.

Samantha could take no more. She headed for the ladies' room, a small single-stall lavatory, where she could have privacy. She brushed past a bewildered Mr. August, who furthered her humiliation by bellowing into the pit, "What's the matter with her?"

16

*H*aley left Samantha, stopped at a sandwich shop to order three ham and cheddar sandwiches, and drove directly to the morgue. She'd been gone all morning. Providing lunch was a goodwill gesture.

It would've worked if it hadn't been for the telephone call from Detective Cluney that came in just as she walked through the door.

"Just in time," Dr. Guthrie blustered.

Haley set the paper lunch bags on the counter by the coffee machine. "What's up?"

"Another body on Hanover. In a ditch near Battery. Same modus operandi as Keating."

"Are you going?" Haley wasn't sure why she asked that. Dr. Guthrie didn't like to be inconvenienced.

"No. You can do it. Too damn humid for my liking."

A true Englishman, the weather in Boston was too damn cold, too damn hot, or too damn humid. Rainy days were acceptable but still warranted a complaint. The "pavement", the British way to say sidewalk, was too damn slippery.

Haley took a minute to collect her sandwich, took a large bite, then grabbed her medical kit. She stared over her shoulder at Mr. Martin. "Would you like to assist?"

Mr. Martin snatched his and Haley's lunch bags as he took long strides in her direction. "Love to, Doc."

By the time they'd traversed the long hallways of the hospital and arrived at Haley's DeSoto, Mr. Martin had finished his lunch. He held up Haley's bag. "Want me to drive?"

Haley hesitated. She didn't like to let other people drive her car, but then her stomach growled loudly. She tossed Mr. Martin the keys, and he lobbed her her lunch bag.

"Good catch," Mr. Martin said with a grin.

"That was nothing," Haley said, sliding into the passenger seat. "I played ball with three brothers. Now, do you even know how to drive?"

"I grew up on a farm too. My pa bought one of the first motorized tractors on the market."

Mr. Martin worked the double-clutch system with

finesse, and Haley rested easy. She dug into her sandwich.

Detective Cluney and his officers were already at the scene. Haley spotted Officer Bell, who looked sheepish and kept his gaze averted. Jack had his back to her, preoccupied with his camera and snapping pictures. He smiled when he spotted her.

"Hello, Dr. Higgins."

"Officer Thompson," Haley returned. "Detective Cluney. What do we have here?"

Both officers stepped aside, and Detective Cluney said, "See for yourself."

The body—on its side, throat cut—lacked blood pools, which pointed to movement to this location after the fact. Haley recognized the man.

"It's Douglas Mulryan," she said. "The secretary at St. Stephen's Church." She crouched down for a closer look. "How odd that a body of a non-member of St. Stephen's was deposited in the church and the church secretary here."

"Seems random, at first glance," Detective Cluney said.

"Who found the body?" Haley asked.

"I did," Officer Bell said. "Just out on the beat."

Convenient, Haley thought. But if Officer Bell was complicit, why would he bring the body to the attention of the police? To keep from becoming suspect himself?

"You get around, Officer Bell," Haley said.

Detective Cluney eyed her keenly. "What do you mean by that?"

"A friend and I were perusing Long Wharf at the docks earlier today, and we saw Officer Bell there."

Tom Bell jumped to his own defense and addressed Detective Cluney's questioning look. "A call about suspicious persons came in, sir."

Haley snorted then turned it into a sneeze. "Oh, sorry. Uh, were we the suspicious persons?"

"It is unlikely to see ladies such as yourselves there, Dr. Higgins."

"But surely we weren't enticing enough to merit a call to the police department. It wasn't like we were prowling. The workers and managers there know police time is valuable and not to be wasted."

"Actually, now that I think about it," Officer Bell said, "gender wasn't mentioned."

Haley glanced about for Officer Harris, but he wasn't there. She was glad to see Mr. Martin was busy taking notes. Her attention returned to the victim. There was a difference between this body and the others. Mr. Mulryan's hands were baby-bottom soft, and from Haley's cursory check, he didn't sport a tattoo.

She looked up and asked, "Can I move him?"

Detective Cluney stared at Jack Thompson. "You done?"

Jack nodded. "Got a full roll."

Haley gently turned the deceased onto his back.

"Cause and time of death, Doctor?" Detective Cluney asked.

"The slice to his neck is the most likely cause." Haley checked the limbs for rigor. "Stiffness is just starting to set in. I'd say eight to ten hours."

"Can I check the pockets?" Detective Cluney asked.

Haley nodded.

The hefty detective squatted with a grunt and then fished through the dead man's pockets. "Nothin'. Whoever dumped him, must've made sure they were empty."

Detective Cluney instructed Tom Bell to check the grounds for possible evidence, and Haley waited until the officer was out of earshot.

Jack Thompson noticed her hesitation. "Is something wrong?"

Haley looked at Jack and glanced at Detective Cluney. "I overheard Will Delaney threaten Mr. Mulryan."

"He said he was going to kill him?" Detective Cluney asked.

"Not specifically. He said that Mr. Mulryan had two days. The threat was implied."

"When was this?" Jack asked.

"Sunday evening after mass."

Detective Cluney worked his thick lips. "So, two days ago?"

Haley nodded. "It looks to me as if Mr. Delaney followed through on his threat."

17

To Samantha's horror, long black streaks of mascara traced down her cheeks. She stared at her reflection, engulfed in a new wave of mortification. This was what she'd looked like while screaming her head off at Mr. Hall. No wonder they snickered behind her back.

With her palms braced against the sink, she let her knees buckle. She had to get herself together. She was stronger than this! And smarter than *them*!

Her silent rally failed to buoy her. No matter what she said or did, she couldn't escape Seth. Even though the courts might grant her a divorce based on Seth's blatant abandonment, the fact that he'd returned would probably be enough cause to overrule it. She'd have to prove cruelty or adultery, or possibly mental illness, but Seth wouldn't take those accusations lying down.

And there was always her daughter to think about. She had no way of protecting Talia from her father.

Samantha let out a long breath, then took off her hat and gloves. She removed her hairpins and with long painted fingernails, combed through her hair and repinned it into a long bob as best as she could without a brush. After that, she turned on the taps and washed her face, but unfortunately, the spare makeup items she carried in her messenger bag had been left in the pit. She checked her pockets and sighed with relief at the discovery of an old lipstick. The surface of the *Tangerine Twist* was worn to almost nothing, but with her fingertip, Samantha mined enough out of the tarnished tube with her pinky finger to cover her washed-out-looking lips.

There wasn't much else she could do besides pin her hat back on and pull on her gloves. With her shoulders back, she headed to Mr. August's office. There was only one choice left for her.

She found Archie August with his usual cigar in his mouth and a plume of blue smoke circling around his head. His large desk was covered with papers and newspapers, the *Boston Daily Record* along with all the competitive rags. He stared up at her over his typewriter.

"Look, Miss Hawke, we all have our bad days. Let's just forget it and move on, huh?"

"I'm afraid it's not that simple." Samantha stepped into the editor's office uninvited and sat tentatively on the edge of one of the chairs that faced her boss.

"My husband came back."

Archie August stilled then slowly moved the cigar from his mouth. "I thought he was dead."

"So did I, but believe me, he's very much alive."

The editor delivered the butt of his cigar to the overfilled ashtray. "I see." He leaned back in his chair and threaded his thick fingers over his belly.

Samantha continued. "He doesn't want me to work."

Mr. August hummed. "Yes, well, I suppose he's got a point, now that you're a married woman again and not a widow."

"I'm in the middle of a potentially big story. I'll have to pass it on to Mr. Milwaukee."

"What's the story?"

"Illegal fight clubs moving about the city to escape detection and litigation."

His bushy brow jumped an inch. "How'd you stumble upon that?"

"That body at St. Stephen's."

The brow flattened. "Right. Yes, give it to Milwaukee. Fight clubs isn't something a lady should get involved with anyway."

Samantha held her tongue. No point in leaving on a bad note by getting into an argument she wouldn't win with her boss.

"Who do you suggest I give the ladies' pages to? I got no ladies left?"

"Does it have to be a lady?" Samantha said.

Mr. August grunted. "From what I've heard, other rags hire men to cover their fluff."

"Maybe Mr. Owen?" Samantha offered. The unassuming Max Owen was a gifted photographer, and Samantha suspected a keen observer. He'd probably enjoy keeping busy with the lighter side to life after covering the darker parts of humanity with Johnny.

"Not a bad idea." Mr. August stood and approached Samantha with an outstretched hand. "I wish you well, Miss Hawke, or, uh, should I say, Mrs. Rosenbaum. It's been a pleasure."

Samantha fought back another round of tears. "Thank you, sir. The pleasure has been all mine."

Johnny wasn't at his desk when Samantha returned. Ignoring the other men in the room who pretended not to notice her, she wrote Johnny a quick note and placed it and her file on Keating on his desk.

She then addressed the room. "I'm leaving, and I won't be returning."

Max Owen stared back with wide eyes. Fred Hall's lips twitched upwards.

"Thank you for allowing me to be a part of your team. Good luck."

Samantha collected her messenger bag and camera —it belonged to her and not the paper—and swallowed a hard lump as she left. She was doing the right thing for Talia.

She was.

18

Samantha caught the next bus, but she didn't go home. Before she went back to being a housewife and spending long hours fighting for territory with Bina, she had one more stop to make. She watched without seeing through the grimy window as busy Bostonians went about their business. When the bus got to the corner of Allen and Charles, she filed off with the other passengers and walked the rest of the way to the hospital.

Saying goodbye to Haley would be hard. She'd probably say they would remain friends, but at best, they might remain friendly, should they ever have reason to see each other again. Samantha's world in the tenements—somehow even with Seth's boast about money, she didn't think they'd escape living there—being a mother, wife, daughter-in-law, and following

Jewish holidays, couldn't possibly coincide with Haley's life. They were friends because their jobs gave a commonality. Take that away, and the rest went with it.

If she was anything, Samantha was a realist. She'd give herself this one day to mourn her losses and be sad, but tomorrow, she'd rise to her new challenge. Being there when Talia needed her was the best silver lining.

Her heels echoed on the hard tiles and steps that went to the basement morgue. She inhaled, and when she forced a smile her face felt tight.

She could do this.

Samantha knocked. Haley's voice called her to come in, and she pushed the door open.

"Samantha?" Haley said with a look of surprise. She wore a white laboratory coat and sat at a side table with a pen in her hand poised over a notepad.

"Hi. Am I interrupting? I can come back." She couldn't, really, but, as she'd hoped, Haley didn't turn her away.

"Of course not. Come in." Haley stood and offered a chair.

Haley was subtle, but Samantha could tell she was assessing Samantha's look and mood.

"I'll make coffee."

. . .

Samantha was thankful for the extra minutes of what she was already mentally referring to as "her old life". She found a small comfort watching Haley prep and plug in the aluminum percolator.

While they waited, Haley asked, "How did it go with your husband?"

Samantha knew that Haley had witnessed her conflict with Seth. From her peripheral, she knew the DeSoto hadn't moved.

"I've quit my job."

Haley raised a dark brow. "That was fast."

"Not fast enough for Seth."

"How do you feel about that? I thought you loved your job?"

"I do. I did, but it's fine, though. I'm fine."

Haley stared back with a look that said she wasn't convinced. The coffee was ready, and Haley poured for them both and added cream and sugar without asking.

She handed the milky brew to Samantha and said, "You look pale. This will help."

Samantha sipped with appreciation. Bina was too cheap to buy either sugar or cream, only milk. Or rather, Bina was good at budgeting pennies, and they couldn't afford luxuries on Samantha's wage.

No longer her problem. See? The lining was getting more silver all the time.

"What about the case?" Haley asked.

"I've given the story to Johnny, with Mr. August's blessing. You don't mind if he calls you occasionally?"

Samantha noted Haley's hesitation before her friend nodded. "Whatever works."

"Where's Mr. Martin?" Samantha asked. The intern was usually around, but Samantha didn't ask for that reason. She was simply trying to make conversation.

"He's in class."

"Right," Samantha said. "Final year of medical school, I think you said."

"That's right."

"And Dr. Guthrie?"

Haley's eyes rolled ever so slightly. "I believe he's engaged with my housekeeper. Tea and crumpets or some such thing."

Samantha chuckled. "I'll miss watching the blooming romance."

"Don't worry," Haley said. "I'll keep you posted."

Silence dropped when they both realized that was probably not true.

"Talia will be happy," Haley said. "Does she know?"

"Not yet." How could she? Seth had only just given Samantha the ultimatum. Haley's eyes flashed with discomfort as if she knew she'd said the wrong thing.

Samantha suddenly felt the need to hurry through her coffee. Her gaze left Haley's face and found an excuse to scan the room. It was then that she noticed a body on one of the autopsy tables. She was off her game—how had she missed that?

"Who's the guy on the table?"

"Another John Doe, on Hanover again. They're dropping like flies now. Dr. Guthrie actually had to go to the scene of the crime this time." Haley's lip twitched into a near grin. "Almost the same modus operandi as Keating. By the way, the blood samples I picked up at the docks match Keating."

"So that was the scene of the crime?"

"The first crime. I just put Douglas Mulryan in the fridge."

"The church secretary?"

Haley nodded. "His body was dropped on the east end of Hanover by the docks."

"Delaney came through on his threat?"

"That's a good possibility."

Samantha wanted to ask more questions, but why should she now that she was no longer an investigative reporter?

Apparently, Haley was determined to tell her

anyway. Anything was better than this dead conversation they were having.

"Evidence of fighting," Haley started, motioning to the body on the slab. "Dumped, but positioned on his side. Cause of death for both was a knife to the throat."

"You said almost the same modus operandi?"

Haley gave her a strange look. "This guy had a fig tucked in his left cheek."

"Put there after the fact," Samantha started, "or was he in the middle of a snack?"

"The latter. It was quite masticated. Just odd, since a trace of fig was at the other dumping site." Haley got to her feet. "I found something else that may be of some importance." She went to the corpse and shifted the sheet until the man's bicep was exposed, then pointed to an ink mark on the underside.

Samantha stared at Haley with a slack jaw.

"What is it?"

"Seth has that same tattoo in the exact same spot."

19

When Samantha left Haley at the morgue, she fought feelings of being bereaved. Life had a way of handing out lemons, but she would make lemonade, goldarn it, starting with picking up Talia from school for a change.

Bina didn't seem surprised to see Samantha when she returned in mid afternoon.

"Seth made me quit my job."

"It's for the best," Bina said. Of course, she would side with her son. Samantha sighed. Maybe, in this case, she was right.

When Samantha announced, "I'm picking up Talia up from school," Bina simply nodded. Samantha felt a flash of sympathy for her mother-in-law. She'd suffered a lot of shock and pain in her life, losing her husband, several children in their infancy, and then

Seth. Now that he was back, Bina should have been brimming with joy, but the wrinkle lines on her face pulled downwards. Even through Bina's rosy lenses, she could see that the son that had left wasn't the son that had returned.

"Where is he?" Samantha asked. The apartment was so small you could practically see into every room from the front door.

"He never said. Just 'out'." Bina shrugged a bony shoulder. "I'm his mama who waited years for him to come home, and all I get is 'out'."

Samantha sauntered wearily into her bedroom and dropped her messenger bag and Kodak to the floor. At least, she wouldn't have to lug those things around anymore. A small purse would do.

Then again, she didn't want Seth to get any ideas about pawning her camera off, and swooped it up. She'd have to find a good place to hide it, but for now, deeply under the bed would have to do.

Samantha changed her clothes and shoes to something simpler, more fitting for a housewife than a career girl, and then left for the school.

The kids were playing in the small playground, and Samantha recognized Talia's blond curls in the midst. She and her friend Sarah were sitting on a flat stone, quietly waiting.

Samantha was about to call for her when, to her

shock, she saw Seth on the perimeter watching Talia too. Was he here to pick her up as well? Without letting Bina know? What if he'd taken Talia before Samantha had gotten here? She'd have been sick with worry.

Samantha approached Seth with every intention of setting him on his way. If she wasn't allowed to work, then she'd be the one to pick their daughter up.

Plus, and she hated that she thought this, Samantha didn't trust Seth to be alone with Talia. He was too coarse for the child's sensitive spirit, and she didn't know what kind of ne'er-do-wells he might expose her to.

Then, as if to prove her judgements against her husband right, a muscular and sinewy man in a sharp-looking suit, joined him. Samantha impulsively ducked behind a milk truck. She didn't want Seth to catch her spying on him. The man with him wore a hat bill tipped low, sunglasses that concealed his eyes, and had his chin tucked low. His back was turned to Samantha, and she couldn't make out his features.

Seth and the man stood in front of the truck and lit up cigarettes. The vehicle acted as a shield and Samantha shimmied quietly around one side, just close enough to hear snippets of what they were saying.

"The boss is wonderin' why you're back," the man said, his voice low and gravelly.

"I figured enough time has passed. Besides, I can't stand the South. Bunch of rednecks."

Samantha thought that was rich, coming from Seth. He wasn't exactly the most sophisticated type.

"And I gotta kid, ya know. A girl, it turns out. Was hopin' it was a boy, but you get what you get, eh?"

Samantha scowled. Seth had known she was expecting when he took off, but he hadn't stuck around long enough to see Talia born.

"And my wife," Seth continued, "she's a looker, eh? I gotta keep her in line. Can't do that from Alabama."

"Sure, whatever, Rosenbaum. Look, the boss says if you're going to kick around Boston, you gotta do your part. Stay in the game."

"Ain't my first rodeo. I took care of the Keatings, dinn't I?"

What did he mean, took care of the Keatings? Samantha's heart almost stuttered to a stop. What did he *mean*?

"He wants to see you."

"Now? I'm getting my kid."

"I thought you said your wife was gonna do it."

Seth shrugged and dropped his cigarette and smashed it with the toe of his boot. "Fine. Let's go."

The two men walked away. Where were they going? Who was the "boss" the stranger spoke of? If only she didn't have to pick up her daughter, she'd trail them. She let out a grunt of frustration.

Once Seth was gone, Samantha stepped back onto the sidewalk and strolled to her daughter. She raised an arm to flag her. "Talia?"

Talia looked up with wide blue eyes. "Mommy? Why are you here?"

Samantha put on a smile. "I wanted to surprise you." She greeted Talia's friend. "Hello, Sarah."

"Hello, Mrs. Rosenbaum."

Samantha reached for Talia's hand. "Ready to go?"

Talia jumped to her feet. "Bye, Sarah."

"How was school?" Samantha asked. One part of her brain paid attention to her daughter's answer, able to ask more questions and offer advice. The other part of her mind worked furiously to figure out what Seth was up to.

There was only one way to find out. The next chance she got, she would follow him.

BINA HEATED up leftover kugel casserole—the pureed potato, egg, and onion dish smelling as delectable as it did freshly made. Around the table, Samantha sat across from Seth, and Talia opposite Bina.

"Will you say the blessing, son?" Bina asked.

Seth wrinkled his nose. "You go ahead, Eema."

Bina's eyes briefly flashed with disappointment before she closed them and began, "*Barukh ata Adonai Eloheinu Melekh ha'olam shehakol nih'ye bidvaro.*" Blessed are You, Lord our God, King of the Universe, through whose word everything comes into being.

"It's so good to have the four of us together again," Bina said, beaming, her motherly blinders back in position. She dished a portion of the casserole onto Seth's plate. "Such a lovely family!"

"It's sho' good to be back," Seth said.

To Samantha, it sounded as if a southern drawl had snuck into his voice. She smiled at her husband. "Where were you all these years, Seth? Alabama?"

Seth's gaze jerked up. "What makes you say that?"

"Oh, nothing." Samantha wasn't about to give away her hand.

Seth answered with a full mouth. "It don't matter where I was, only that I'm back." He swallowed and stared hard. "Got that, sugarplum?" He turned his attention on his daughter. "Hey, Talia, what grade are you in?"

"First."

"So, I didn't miss too much."

Only the first six years of her life!

He grinned crookedly at Samantha as if reading her mind. "I'm not much for diapers and baby talk."

Bina brought out a plate of her famed rugalach—a

rich pastry filled with fruit and nuts. This kind of thing was considered too extravagant or expensive during such depressive times, and was usually only made on Talia's birthday. Bina, ignoring Samantha's frown, declared, "We're celebrating!"

Samantha offered the sweet tea Bina insisted on serving and passed a teacup to Seth. He winked at her, produced a flask from his boot and poured amber fluid into his. Samantha quickly looked to Talia, relieved that her daughter hadn't witnessed the sleight of hand.

Finally, the affair ended. Samantha excused Talia to play in their room. Seth turned on the radio and poured himself more "tea" as he got comfortable on the couch. Samantha helped Bina clean up, feeling disturbed by Bina's uncharacteristic whistling along to "Happy Days are Here Again".

Samantha dried the last dish and put it away. She intended to hide away with Talia, but Seth, catching her off guard, stopped her in the short hallway.

"Babe. The couch is really uncomfortable." He placed an arm on the wall just to the left of her head. He leaned in and whispered. "I want to sleep in my bed tonight. With my wife."

Samantha weakly protested. "But, Talia . . ."

"I'll make her a room in the attic."

"The attic?" Samantha was incredulous. The only way to get to the attic was through the fire escape.

She'd used the uninhabited space to develop photos in the past, but it wasn't fit for a child.

"It's unsuitable. She'll be afraid."

"Then she can sleep with Eema. Samantha, a man has a right to sleep with his own wife."

"Give me one more night with her. I need to explain things. And maybe you should let your mother know."

Seth pushed himself off the wall. "Fine. One more night on the couch, but that's it."

"Okay."

Samantha hurried to her room and closed the door behind her.

"Are you okay, Mommy?" Talia asked. Her eyes were round and filled with uncertainty. Samantha's heart swelled with love for her daughter, and there was nothing, *nothing*, she wouldn't do for her. The only things that mattered—keep Talia safe and try to make her happy.

"Of course, sweetie." She sat on the bed beside Talia and stroked her silky hair. "Daddy and I were just talking, and now that he's back, well, he doesn't want to keep sleeping on the couch, and this bed is too small for all three of us." Samantha chuckled as she tried to keep it light. "So we thought, wouldn't it be fun for you to share a room with Bubba."

Talia wrinkled her nose. "I don't want to move in with Bubba."

"It won't be that bad. And maybe, after a while, Daddy will move us into a bigger place, and you can have your own room."

Why had she said that?

Samantha didn't believe it for a second, but a little hope in times like this didn't hurt.

"I don't want my own room, Mommy. I like things the way they are."

"I know. Let's not think about it right now. I'm still here for tonight."

Samantha read a chapter of *Anne of Avonlea*, said a Christian prayer, then tucked Talia in with a kiss on the forehead. "Go to sleep, angel."

Talia fought the inevitable for as long as she could, but soon she'd drifted into dreamland. Samantha, hoping she wasn't too late, tiptoed into the living room. Asleep in a sitting position, Seth's legs sprawled, his head tilted back, and his mouth stayed opened.

Bina exited from the only bathroom, looking like an elf in her oversized housecoat, worn slippers, and gray hair wrapped in a headband. "Goodnight, Samantha," she said. A peek into the living room caused the elderly woman to go directly to her bed. Samantha got ready too, but she didn't dress in her nightie. She brushed her teeth and pinned her hair up. She put on a black skirt and blouse and tucked her blond tresses under a black hat, hoping she'd blend into the darkness outside. Seth had been gone most of the night the evening before, and Samantha counted on him to do the same again tonight.

All she had to do was wait.

20

Haley fished through the files of all corpses that had come through the morgue with a tattoo and looked for anything that might help her to connect the dots. It couldn't be a coincidence that the Keating brothers, the new John Doe, and Seth Rosenbaum all had the same tattoo. There had to be a connection, and several other similar deaths seemed to support her hypothesis.

Mr. Martin walked in and stared at the piles of files on the table.

"Can I help with something?"

Haley explained her tattoo dilemma. "I've found three other decedents who died in the last five years with the same tattoo. All suspicious deaths and none solved. I suspect that illicit fighting is the connection between them."

"What's the tattoo look like?"

Haley produced a photograph from one of the files. "It's two spiders entangled, about the size of a quarter on the inside wrist of the right hand."

Mr. Martin's brow buckled in thought. "I've seen that symbol before."

"Do you remember who?"

"Not a who. A where. Occasionally, it pops up on a door frame or lamp post. I saw it for myself when I picked up my cousin who works on the docks."

"On Long Wharf?" Haley said.

The intern nodded. "Spider fighting is an actual betting event. Common in prisons, at least according to my cousin." He shrugged a shoulder. "Our family's black sheep. Maybe they're using it as a way to let fighters and bettors know where the next fight is."

Haley continued the thought. "By moving the fights around the city, they make it difficult to get caught and to be shut down."

"Exactly."

What bothered Haley about this line of thought was that Joe hadn't had a tattoo. It was the one thing about the modus operandi of these more recent murders that didn't connect with him. Haley felt a deep sense of despair. She'd hoped that by solving this case, she'd solve her brother's as well. Was his case destined to remain unsolved forever?

Haley gathered up the files. "We need to find the next location."

Mr. Martin wrinkled his nose. "That's like looking for a needle in a haystack."

Haley was about to agree when a new thought came to her. "Maybe not."

AFTER A QUICK DINNER WITH MOLLY, who talked excitedly about going to the theater with Dr. Guthrie, Haley prepared for her own evening. It involved dressing in comfortable slacks, low-heeled pumps, and tying her hair back in a ponytail. A hat wasn't necessary, but she did put on a pair of black gloves. In a small purse, which she wore diagonally over her shoulders, she placed a flashlight, a set of lock picks—just in case —and her H&R pistol.

She could very well be on a wild goose chase. Her most significant lead was the presence of figs on or near two of the most recent murders. Her gut told her that people working at the Fruit Company warehouse on Long Wharf or areas nearby set up the fights. There were several warehouses on the wharf, and Haley hoped she'd come across the fighting in one of them. All she had to do was find the symbol of the battling spiders.

Her trek could lead to nothing more than a late-night walk in an industrial area, but either way, it was dangerous for a woman alone at night, and she had to be exceedingly diligent.

Driving at night was always an adventure. A string of big bug-eye lights rumbled on rough streets under low-hanging streetlights. She passed couples out for dinner, and ruffians out for trouble. At least the number of vehicles on the road was fewer, and in no time, Haley parked along Atlantic Avenue near Long Wharf.

Dark hair was an asset when it came to staying hidden in the dark, but white skin could prove troublesome. The half moon shone, but the clouds moved in and out causing a slow-motion effect due to intermittent flashes of light. Haley kept her head down and trod stealthily.

She wasn't the only one skulking about. Besides the mice and rats, men came out of nowhere in ones and twos, then disappeared again near the end of the dock. Haley's pulse jumped. Were they looking for a fight to bet on?

Using her flashlight sparingly, Haley kept close to the row of warehouses as she searched for the fighting spiders image. She thought she'd missed it when she reached the end of the dock and still hadn't seen it. The sound of a man's shoes slapping the roadway caused Haley to duck out of sight. From her position, she could see the man's face, and she scowled. Seth Rosenbaum up to no good again. He disappeared between two warehouses, and Haley, confident he'd just shown her the way, was just about to step in behind him when she spotted another form, female this time, and very familiar.

Haley quickly shone her flashlight at the figure and then pulled it away. She whispered, "Hawke, it's me."

Samantha stared back in astonishment. Haley waved her over before someone else spotted her standing there.

"What are you doing here?" Samantha whispered.

"Probably the same thing you are," Haley whispered back. "I saw Seth dart down that breezeway."

"I decided to follow him," Samantha said. "I know he's my husband, but I don't trust him. He won't tell me where he's been or what he's been doing. I need to know the truth."

Haley understood. "Follow me and stay close."

Like alley cats, they eased behind parked trucks until they reached the area where Seth had disappeared. Haley's flashlight beam landed on a small sign with two embattled spiders etched onto it tacked to the side of the warehouse. Haley nodded at Samantha.

They found an obscure handle to a door closed tightly.

"Should we go in?" Samantha asked.

"Let's take a peek first." Haley tried the knob which was unlocked, and inched the door open. Inside, a group of men circled two fighters. Their backs were turned, and they didn't notice Haley and Samantha slip inside. Providing a suitable hiding spot, large crates had been pushed out of the way to make room for the makeshift ring.

It was challenging to identify who was fighting since the fighters kept their fists up to protect their faces. The men fought shirtless with bare knuckles. Eventually a blow would be struck, but the cheering men, shuffling on their feet, prevented a clear view.

Then the moment of alignment happened: the crowd seemed to split, which gave Haley and Samantha a line of sight. One of the fighters threw a punch and hit the other straight on the jaw. The one who'd been hit dropped his fists as he fell to the floor, his face revealed.

Samantha gasped. Seth was down for the count.

21

*K*nowing Haley, Samantha hadn't been too surprised to find that her friend had somehow tracked the fight club location. If she ever had a chance, she'd ask how, but watching Seth take a hit, which, from her viewpoint behind the crates, looked damaging and possibly fatal, she could think of nothing but Seth's body on the dirty wooden floor.

Get up, get up, get up!

She wasn't the only one with the sentiment, though the men who'd bet on Seth to win weren't caring.

"Get up, you scoundrel!"

"Stay down, and I'll kill you myself."

"Serves me right for betting on a Jew!"

Samantha took an impulsive step toward her fallen husband, only to be suddenly jerked back.

"No," Haley said sharply. "We have to get out of here before anyone sees us."

"But Seth—"

"There's a phone booth on Atlantic. We can call for an ambulance."

Seth moaned and lifted one shoulder. Good, he wasn't dead. It was all she needed to know to come to her senses. Haley was right. If they were discovered there, it would be a disaster. The question was how to get away unnoticed? The stack of crates that concealed them in the dim light was at least three steps from the door. It was one thing to sneak in when everyone was facing the fight, but now the men were pivoting to complain to their companions, their peripheral visions aligned with the door.

Samantha felt a poke in the ribs, and then saw Haley pointing with the same finger.

"Harris," Haley mouthed.

Samantha scowled. And then her heart dropped into her stomach. Harris stepped aside, and clear as day stood Tom Bell.

Two thugs lifted Seth to his feet and braced him up. They headed for the door, forcing Samantha and Haley to shuffle to the other side of the crates. To Samantha's dismay, Seth was tossed outside, but at least it looked like he'd regained his footing.

Stupid man! What had he gotten himself into?

The winner of the match returned to the middle of the room, and a new contestant was presented. This captured the attention of the crowd, which allowed Samantha and Haley to escape. They moved around the crates toward the door but stilled suddenly when a shadow blocked the light.

A man whispered harshly. "What are you two doing here?"

"Tom?" Samantha said. "How—?"

"I'm working a case. I'm the only sober guy in the room. If Har— If anyone sees you—please, you're in extreme danger."

A man behind them coughed loudly. Tom spun on his heel, effectively concealing them.

"Hey, buster," Tom said. "Done with the fight already?"

"My guy lost," the said with another round of coughing. "Hey, do you got a cig?"

Tom produced one and handed it to the guy.

"Thanks, mister."

Samantha let out a breath.

Tom joined them again.

"Is there another way out?" Haley asked.

Tom stepped forward. "Follow me."

They passed several interior doors that Samantha assumed were offices, until a dark hallway presented itself. Tom hurried them along until they reached an exterior door. It locked from the inside, and Tom shifted the latch and opened it.

"Do you know your way from here?" he said. "I'd come with you, but a sudden absence on my part would cause suspicion."

"My car is at the end of the dock," Haley said. "We'll be careful."

Tom nodded with a look of apprehension. He hesitated as if debating his choice, then disappeared back inside.

"Let's go," Haley said.

Amidst the roar of the traffic inland and the crashing of the waves in the harbor, they plodded silently, keeping to the shadows of the parked commercial trucks. Samantha kept a lookout for Seth, but he was nowhere. She just hoped that she could get home before he did, or at least, that he'd be passed out on the couch in a deep enough slumber not to hear her sneak back in.

THE NEXT MORNING, Haley felt compelled to go back to the site of the first body drop at St. Stephen's church. She hated how stuck this investigation felt, and worse, she was convinced that the key to the case would unlock the mystery of her brother's death.

Haley scoured the grounds of the church, which,

unlike many church plots, was mostly an alley between buildings and a short patch of grass along the front. This time there was nothing unusual, no small bits of boot dirt or scraps of ripped clothing, nothing as easy as that.

The streets, like every other day, were filled with darkly painted square-backed vehicles and dotted with pedestrians in a hurry. The overcast sky produced gloomy shadows. Everyone went about their business like it was just another ordinary day, oblivious to the darker side of the city where murders happened and murderers went unpunished.

"Can I help you, miss?"

Haley turned toward the kind voice of Father O'Hara. He looked slimmer in his cassock than he did when he wore the surplice during mass. Dressed in his black suit with the distinguishing white collar, he approached, and then his thick gray eyebrows jumped with recognition. "Dr. Higgins. I'm sorry. I didn't recognize you at first." He smiled broadly. "My eyesight's not what it once was."

"That's quite all right, Father O'Hara," Haley said. She reached out and shook the priest's hand. "Forgive me for traipsing about. I hope you don't mind my trespassing."

"It's hardly trespassing when it's the Lord's house in question."

"I'm still trying to work out the deaths of the man found on the grounds and of Mr. Mulryan."

"Yes, yes, dear me, such a tragedy. I've prayed for their souls."

Haley smiled softly at the sentiment.

"Do you have any reason to believe that Mr. Mulryan and Mr. Keating knew each other?"

Father O'Hara tilted his head. "Beyond warming a pew inside?"

"Yes."

"I couldn't really say. Despite what people might think, I'm not privy to everyone's private affairs."

"But surely you must know something. Anything that could help the case? Bring justice to these men? There must be gossip or other ways of hearing news?"

Father O'Hara frowned, and Haley knew that he understood what she was insinuating. Had he heard anything in the confessional? Not that he could tell her if he had.

His smile returned, and he asked, "Do you know the story about Judas, Dr. Higgins?"

Haley let out a short breath of frustration at the priest's sudden change of subject. Roman Catholics considered the confessional sacred, and honestly, Haley would've been a little disappointed in the Father had he broken that sacred trust. Still, a little break was all she was asking for.

"Yes, Father O'Hara," she answered. "I would say that most Christians have."

"Everyone knows that Judas betrayed Jesus, but few are aware of how close they were as friends beforehand. Anyway, Dr. Higgins, I have to run. I've promised Mrs. Breen I'd pray for her sick cat." He waved as he strolled away. "Cheers!"

Haley returned with a polite, "Goodbye," and stared after the man as he headed down Hanover Street.

What did he mean by that little anecdote? Was it a hint? A clue? If felt like it might be, but in that case, who betrayed whom?

SAMANTHA WORRIED HER HANDS. Seth hadn't come home after the fight. The couch and neatly folded blankets placed at the end of it by Bina were untouched.

"Where's Daddy?"

Talia, dressed for school in a dress that had one too many patches for Samantha's liking, reached for her mother's hand, a sure sign that the little girl felt uneasy about her father, even though he wasn't present in the room.

"I don't know," Samantha said honestly. "He might've stayed overnight with a friend."

"Like I sometimes do at Sarah's house?"

"Exactly. Now go brush your teeth, and I'll walk you to school."

Spending these extra moments with Talia was a blessing. Usually, Samantha would be rushing out the door to get to work, and Bina would be walking Talia to school.

"Do you really think that?" Bina looked even more frail than usual.

Samantha shrugged. She didn't know how much she should tell Bina. Her instinct was to protect her, much like she was doing with Talia, but Bina wasn't a child, and she deserved to know the truth.

"Let's finish our coffee," she said.

Bina glanced at Samantha then shuffled to her chair and sat. She didn't pick up her coffee mug, only studied Samantha with wary eyes.

Samantha took a sip of her coffee, now grown cold, then began, "I followed him last night. Down to the docks."

Bina stared back with a look of disapproval, but Samantha continued before her mother-in-law could cut her off. "You've heard of illegal fight clubs?"

Appearing to shrink in size, Bina slumped in the chair. "Men fight like chickens, and other men bet on who will get their eyes pecked out." She leaned forward. "Don't tell me—"

"I'm afraid so. Seth was fighting, and he lost. The last time I saw him, a couple of big oafs threw him out the door."

Bina pointed an accusing crooked finger. "You didn't go to help him?"

"I had to make sure I wasn't seen." Samantha purposely left Haley out of the story. "I went out another door, and when I was outside, I tried to find Seth, but he wasn't around."

"Where is he now?"

"I don't know. That part is true."

Samantha pushed away from the table and took the few short steps needed into the living room. She knelt by the couch and pulled out Seth's suitcase.

"What are you doing?" Bina asked.

"Looking for clues."

"It's not right for you to snoop through his things."

Samantha shot her mother-in-law a stern look. "Why not? I'm his wife. He shouldn't keep secrets from me anyway."

It was what Samantha told herself to push back the guilt she felt as she rifled through Seth's personal belongings. His t-shirts and button-up shirts were neatly folded as was an extra pair of trousers. *Seth always did like things to be kept neat and orderly, something he inherited from his mother*, Samantha thought.

Folded underwear, shirts, and pants in need of

ironing. There was a single book, the Torah, which had a place marked. Samantha flipped it open to the beginning of Genesis, but it wasn't the ancient text that caught her eye. It was the bookmark, or rather an old photograph acting as one—a photo of Seth, the way he looked before he had disappeared, youthful and smiley, with his arm around the shoulders of another man in a friendly manner.

Samantha took a closer look and felt the floor move. She recognized the other man. Joe Higgins.

Samantha's husband and Haley's brother had known each other.

She flipped it over to the back and wrinkled her nose in puzzlement. She recognized Seth's handwriting. On the smooth, white surface, he'd scribbled *Dempsey and Carpentier.*

What on earth did that mean?

22

*A*fter a quick check of her wristwatch, Haley rushed to her parked DeSoto. She needed to get to the morgue pronto, or Dr. Guthrie would soon lose patience with her seeming inability to track the time.

As expected, her boss was waiting. He frowned. "Is there a time change I'm not aware of?"

"No, sir," Haley said. "I was double-checking something on the case I'm working on."

"A case not sanctioned or commissioned by the hospital that employs you, I might add."

"I know—"

Dr. Guthrie held up a lined palm. "No excuses. Now a cup of tea would be nice. You know how I like it."

Haley held in a smile. If making Dr. Guthrie

English-style tea was her penance, then she was getting off easily. She put the kettle to boil, measured the tea, and dropped it into a warmed-up pot. While the water heated up, she selected a teacup and saucer, and placed them on a tray along with a bowl of sugar and a small pitcher of milk. When the kettle whistled, she poured the hot water into the teapot, then placed the pot on the tray. Dr. Guthrie liked to pour his own cup, so Haley had only to walk the tray over to the man's office.

"Here you go, Dr. Guthrie," she said with a smile. She placed the tray on one end of the desk, a spot cleared by Dr. Guthrie as she walked over. Haley had teased the pathologist about the constant mess on his desk. He'd grumbled back, "Organized confusion."

"Oh, Dr. Higgins."

Haley paused at the door. "Yes?"

"How is your investigation going? In case I need to advocate for you in the future, I might as well know."

"It's rather frustrating, to be honest," Haley admitted. "I feel like a rat on a wheel, always running but never finding the cheese."

"Are you sure it's your calling? Perhaps you should leave such matters to the police."

"I am leaving all matters to the police. If you recall, Detective Cluney asked for my assistance this time."

"Righto. Well then, I'm sure the puzzle will

present a solution in good time." He waved long fingers in dismissal.

Haley turned and rolled her eyes. What did Molly see in this gruff old man? Beauty lay in the eyes of the beholder.

Returning to her desk, Haley sat, leaned back, and put her feet on her desk. She closed her eyes and folded her hands in front of her. Maybe if she just relaxed, let her mind go, the puzzle would *present a solution.*

If only she didn't have a stack of paperwork waiting for her attention. Haley sighed and brought her feet back to the floor. And just in time, too, as a knock on the door was followed by the entrance of Samantha Rosenbaum.

Haley noted the circles under Samantha's eyes and the uncharacteristic slouch of her shoulders. She also wasn't used to seeing the journalist dressed so casually. She approached Haley's desk wearing a faded day dress.

"How are you this morning?" Haley asked. "Is everything all right?"

Samantha took a wooden chair that sat to the side of Haley's desk and stared back with a look of worry.

"Seth didn't come home last night," she finally said. "I'm worried something's happened to him."

Haley didn't make light of Samantha's concern.

She only hoped that Seth Rosenbaum would not be the next body to show up on Hanover Street.

"Have you contacted the police?" Haley asked.

"Not yet." Samantha paused, then added, "I wanted to talk to you first. I have something to show you, and I'll warn you, it's going to be a bit of a shock."

Haley felt a tingle of consternation. "What is it?"

Samantha slipped her fingers into her dress pocket then produced a small photograph. She handed it to Haley.

"That's Seth when he was younger."

Haley couldn't keep from gulping. Samantha was right—she was shocked. She stared back at her friend. "They knew each other?"

Samantha nodded. "Read the back. I don't understand what it means."

Haley turned the photograph over. "Dempsey and Carpentier."

"I've never heard of the names," Samantha said.

Haley squinted back. "Dempsey and Carpentier are boxers. Champions. They fought together in July of twenty-one. My dad, brothers, and I listened to the fight on the radio."

The memory crushed Haley's heart. The radio had been brand new, a luxury her family could ill afford, but her pa had insisted. "The world is changing and stuck out on this farm, this machine is our only way to know what's goin' on out there." It was an excuse, since newspapers had been doing a fine job of delivering the news until then. He, like Haley and her brothers, had been a sports buff. Their mother only shook her head and busied herself with her rosebushes.

When the Heavyweight Championship took place in July of '21, Haley, her pa, and brothers circled around the big radio with their ears attuned. Her ma had made sugar cookies, and Haley and Joe fought over the last one, which resulted in it breaking into crumbs on the floor.

"Now you gone and dun it," young Joseph had said. He'd tried to sound angry, but Haley could see the twinkle in his eye.

"Something for the mouse family," she'd said.

Pa had shushed them with a firm shake of his head. Only Haley had even noticed when the mice stuck their pink noses out of the hole along the baseboard.

"Who won?" Samantha asked, breaking Haley out of her reverie.

"Dempsey. I don't know why Seth would've written those names on the back of a photograph of him and Joe."

The telephone rang, and Haley answered. She covered the receiver and mouthed toward Samantha. "Tom Bell."

"Hello, Officer," Haley said. "How can I help you?"

"Detective Cluney asked me to call you about Mr. Mulryan's watch. We found a fingerprint on the face of it that didn't belong to its owner."

Haley's interest was ignited. "Whose print was it? Do you know?"

"Yes, Doctor. The print was on file with the department. It belongs to Mr. Seth Rosenbaum."

23

Samantha could tell by the look on Haley's face that something was wrong. Her mouth grew dry, and her chest tightened. "What happened?"

Haley set the receiver back on its cradle.

"The police have evidence connecting Seth to Douglas Mulryan. They found his fingerprint on Mr. Mulryan's watch."

Samantha's throat suddenly tightened, and she struggled to swallow.

"Are you okay?" Haley asked. "I'll get you some water."

Samantha was grateful for the pause. Her mind raced. *How on earth had Seth's fingerprint got on Douglas Mulryan's watch? Seth was a lout, but he wasn't a killer.*

Was he?

Seven years ago, Samantha's answer would've been a resounding *no way*. Now, she wasn't so sure.

Haley brought a glass of water, and Samantha took a sip. "Thank you."

"Do you know where he is?" Haley asked softly. She'd returned to her seat and leaned over the desk. "It's imperative to say so if you do."

Samantha shook her head. "I'd tell you if I knew. I wish I did."

Haley worked her lips with a faraway look.

"What are you thinking?"

"About the tattoo. Seth has one. The Keating brothers, and this latest John Doe had one."

"But Douglas Mulryan didn't." Nor did Joe Higgins, but Samantha didn't say it aloud.

"The only other person I've see with that same tattoo," Haley began, "is Will Delaney."

"Do you think Seth's with Mr. Delaney?"

Haley got to her feet. "There's only one way to find out."

Samantha wasn't so quick to follow. "Do you think we should let Tom know?"

Haley gave her a sideways glance. "Do you trust him now?"

"He told you about the fingerprint. He helped us get out of the club. I think he's working the case." Samantha felt foolish now for even suspecting Tom.

He was her friend. He'd only ever helped her when she needed it. And right now, she needed it.

Haley nodded toward the telephone. "I'll let you do the honors."

Samantha knew the number by heart. She dialed the operator and asked to be connected to the police station, then on to Officer Bell.

After several moments, he was on the line. "Bell here."

"Tom, it's Samantha."

"Hi, Samantha. Are you all right?"

"Yes. I just want to tell you that Seth didn't come home after the fight last night. I'm worried he's in trouble."

Tom simply hummed.

Samantha continued. "Dr. Higgins and I think he may contact Will Delaney."

"Oh? Why's that?"

"The two-spider tattoo. Seth has one, and so does Mr. Delaney."

"I'm not going to ask how you know that."

Good, Samantha thought. "Will you go there?"

"As it turns out, luck is on your side. Our men are on the lookout for Seth Rosenbaum. Patrolman Fanning spotted him going into Delaney's building. I'm heading over there right now."

"Great. We'll see you there."

"No, Samantha, don't come. It's too danger—"

Samantha hung up before Tom Bell could finish. She sprang to her feet and stared at Haley. "Let's go."

SAMANTHA AND HALEY remained wordless as Haley drove her car to Delaney's home. Samantha wasn't even sure where that was, but she couldn't bring herself to form the words. She felt as if she were breathing underwater, that even though the world outside the open windows moved quickly, her own experience moved in slow motion. Her world had imploded when Seth had disappeared, but this was worse. Then, she was sad and angry.

Now, she was afraid.

Of what, Samantha couldn't quite say. Seth moving in and them stepping into their old roles of husband and wife had seemed a monumental problem just yesterday. How had it escalated to this? To Seth in hiding once again.

Only this time, he'd be caught. That was the ball of fire in Samantha's stomach. Her husband had done something dreadful, a yet undetermined crime, but something dreadful. She felt it in her bones.

Belatedly, Samantha realized that life as she'd come to know it had been good. Challenging, yes, but comfortable. Predictable.

Her hands shook noticeably as she brushed stray blond wisps of hair off her face. She tucked her hands under her thighs, hoping that Haley hadn't noticed. She tensed further when Haley pulled the DeSoto to a stop in the upper-class area of Beacon Hill.

"Delaney lives here?"

"Penthouse." Haley turned. "I don't know if he's here or not. Do you want to wait in the car?"

Samantha shook her head. "I'm okay."

Outside, near the front of the building, Samantha noticed a familiar form and frowned deeply. "Johnny's here."

"How?" Haley started.

"He must've gotten a tip from the station." Samantha swallowed. "That means Seth is here, and there's going to be an arrest." Samantha sprung out of the car.

Haley shouted after her. "Samantha!"

Samantha ignored Haley's plea, and sprinted to the front entrance. Despite everything, she felt compelled to warn Seth. He *was* her husband after all and Talia's father. To do this she needed to get to the penthouse suite, which meant she had to get past the doorman who saw her coming.

"Miss?"

"That man out there?" Samantha pointed to

Johnny and silently pleaded forgiveness. "He's after me. Please, help!"

The man's face buckled with outrage, and he ran to the door. Samantha wasted no time. While the doorman threatened to call the police on Johnny, Samantha slipped into the elevator. Police sirens could be heard in the distance.

"Penthouse, please." She smiled at the elevator operator and batted her lashes. "Mr. Delaney is waiting for me."

Just as the elevator doors closed, Samantha heard Haley's voice imploring her to stop.

Too late.

She asked the attendant, "How many elevators are in this building?"

"Just the one, ma'am. There's talk of putting in a second one, but it won't go to the penthouse."

"I see." She had some time before Haley, Johnny, and the police made it up. She had mere minutes to work out a plan. Not nearly long enough. The elevator bells announced her arrival at the penthouse floor, and she still had no idea what she would do besides winging it.

"Thank you," Samantha said. She had a coin in her pocket, one she could ill afford to give away, but she presented it to the elevator attendant anyway. She might need his help later.

Samantha had never been to a penthouse suite before and was shocked to discover that the step out of the elevator didn't take her into a hallway, but directly into the suite. Will Delaney sat on a plush settee with his legs crossed and a cigarette hanging out of his mouth. He stared at Samantha with a look of amusement.

"Are you lost, or is this my lucky day?"

"Hello, Mr. Delaney. I don't have a lot of time."

"Fine by me," he said with a seductive smirk. "I can accommodate your schedule."

"You misunderstand. I'm looking for Seth Rosenbaum."

Delaney uncrossed his legs and put out his cigarette. "Who?" he said carelessly. He stood languidly and stepped over to the side table. He glanced over his shoulder. "Thirsty? I have the best Canadian whiskey on hand." He grinned again. "It's a gift from me to you. I won't tell if you won't."

"Please, Mr. Delaney. Seth is my husband. I believe he's in trouble." Samantha debated telling the arrogant man that the police were on their way up, but it was bad enough she was trying to give Seth a tip. As his wife, the law might overlook her misstep, but they wouldn't smile on her interfering with a man known to run illegal fighting.

"Have a drink with me, and then I'll tell you what you want to know."

No time. She shouted, "Seth! Seth!"

Her pleas did the trick. A door cracked open, and Seth walked out. "Sugarplum," he said with a scowl. "You shouldn't be here."

At that moment, when she saw the dark blankness behind his eyes, his soulless, uncaring stare, Samantha knew he was right. With long strides he reached her, grabbed her wrist tightly, and pulled her to himself. Not in a romantic way, but as a shield against attack.

She'd made a big mistake coming alone, and now she would pay for it.

24

*H*aley was astounded by Samantha's behavior. What did she think she would accomplish by going off on her own like that? Get arrested, likely, but hopefully not worse. Haley didn't know Seth Rosenbaum, but she was certain he couldn't be trusted, not even with his own wife's life.

"What the heck?" Johnny Milwaukee brushed the doorman off. "She duped you, man! Where is she now?"

The doorman searched behind him with a look of confusion at not finding Samantha there.

"See?" Mr. Milwaukee said. "She pulled one on you."

By the time Haley and Johnny had made it inside the building and the lobby, the doors of the elevator were closing.

"Wait!" Haley shouted, but it was too late.

She let out a long sigh as the police cruisers pulled up. Officers Bell and Harris hopped out of the first car.

"What are you two doing here?" Tom Bell asked sternly.

"Samantha's gone up," Haley said. "We tried to stop her."

Tom Bell blanched then barked at the doorman. "How many floors?"

"Seven, sir."

"You go on," Johnny said. "I'll wait for the elevator."

"You stay where you are, sir!" Tom returned.

Officer Harris, who appeared to be in good physical shape, stepped in. "I'll take the steps; you get the elevator when it comes. Still might be faster." He raced down the corridor and disappeared.

An unlikely trio, Haley, Mr. Milwaukee, and Officer Bell, waited in silence for the elevator to return to the main floor. The three watched as the arrow ticked down the levels like a clock hand: five, four, three—

"Maybe you should call for back up," Haley suggested.

"We don't even know if Rosenbaum is here," Officer Bell said.

"But he might be," Haley said, "and Samantha could be in trouble."

—Two, one. The elevator doors opened. Officer Bell shouted to the doorman. "Sir, call the station and ask them to send another car on my authority. Officer Tom Bell."

The three squeezed in beside the doorman. Tom pressed against Mr. Milwaukee's arm. "I insist that you stay here," Tom said.

Mr. Milwaukee smiled snidely. "You can't forbid a citizen to ride the elevator."

Officer Bell gave the attendant the go-ahead to engage the lift.

"If you get in my way, I swear I'll arrest you for obstruction of justice," Officer Bell snapped. "You too, Dr. Higgins."

Haley bobbed her head. She just wished she could make this blasted elevator move faster!

The crawl of the elevator made Haley's skin crawl with frustration. Finally, the attendant announced, "Penthouse."

The doors opened, and Haley's heart fell into her stomach. Seth had a neck hold on Samantha.

Seth's eyes darted about the room wildly. "Stay back!"

Samantha whimpered against his grip.

Tom Bell drew his pistol. "Let her go, Rosenbaum!"

Seth dragged Samantha toward the elevator and shouted his demands, "Move yourselves against the wall."

Will Delaney, with his arms limply in the air, shifted to the far wall, the only one to heed Seth's demands. "I swear, I don't know this man," he said. "He broke in somehow, just before you lot."

"Liar!" Samantha cried. "You were at the warehouse on Long Wharf watching him fight. I saw you!"

Seth Rosenbaum and Will Delaney shared a quick look, clearly wondering how Samantha could've known that.

"And he lost," Haley said. "Is that why you had him thrown out, Mr. Delaney? Did Mr. Rosenbaum come to see you today to ask for a second chance?"

"I didn't want a second chance," Seth said. "I wanted to kill him."

"I told you, he's crazy!" Will Delaney said. "A common thief, caught in the act."

Seth jerked in response. "I'll kill you yet!"

Tom Bell had his pistol trained on Seth, but the slightest slip in his aim, and he could shoot Samantha instead. Haley's pulse hammered in her temples. The moment sizzled. One wrong, impulsive move and the situation could become tragic.

"Let Samantha go," Officer Bell said, "and you can take the elevator alone."

Seth grinned. "I'm not stupid. Sam's my insurance."

"She's your wife," Haley said. "You wouldn't want her to get hurt, would you?"

"You leave me to deal with what's mine." Seth tightened his hold on Samantha, which made her squeal. Haley tensed. Mr. Milwaukee and Officer Bell did the same.

Seth yelled, "Git back, I tell ya, or I'll break her neck, and her death will be on your hands!"

The man was clearly unhinged, Haley thought. What had happened to him all those years ago to set him on this path?

"He killed Joe Higgins," Seth said, nodding toward Delaney.

What? The throbbing in Haley's head exploded. She slowly set her gaze on Will Delaney.

"He's lying! He killed Joe Higgins. Joe was a better fighter. Made more money. This idiot here was jealous."

Seth laughed like a maniac. "Joe had infiltrated the fight club and was about to rat to the police and bust it wide open. I saw Delaney kill him with my own eyes."

Was this true? Had Joe been a hero?

"You killed Joe Higgins," Delaney insisted. "Besides, it's your word against mine."

Haley heard herself speak, "If this is true, Mr. Rosenbaum, why did you leave town?"

"Because I didn't want to end up like Joe."

Delaney sniggered. "Because he didn't want to hang."

Haley pressed on, "But you came back."

"I came for justice." Seth's face was red with fury. Haley worried that he might injure Samantha unintentionally.

"Let Samantha go," Haley said.

Bell had his gun on Seth, but it was apparent that he couldn't watch out for Mr. Delaney as well. From the corner of her eye, Haley saw him make a move to the window and out the fire escape.

"I'd stop if I were you," she said. She removed the H&R from her purse. "I don't like to use this, but I'll warn you, I'm a good shot."

"Isn't this just great," Jonny Milwaukee chided. He'd been so quiet, taking it all in, that Haley had almost forgotten the journalist was in the room. "Two with a gun and one with a girl. I feel left out."

"Isn't that your boyfriend?" Seth said. His hold was too tight, Samantha couldn't respond. Seth's common sense appeared to be overridden by jealousy. "Come here," he said to Milwaukee. "If you want her, come get her."

Tom shook his head, "Don't."

"Do it!" Seth screamed. "Come get her!"

Milwaukee, like he didn't have a care in the world, strutted over.

"Don't, Johnny," Samantha said. "I have this."

"I know you do, doll."

Haley blinked in disbelief as Samantha curled her body into Seth's and rolled him over her back. In seconds, Seth was on the floor gasping for breath.

Tom Bell, looking slightly shell-shocked, breathily said, "Samantha?"

Looking both proud and abashed, Samantha stared back at them. "Mr. Milwaukee taught me how, after our last case."

Johnny Milwaukee's grin curled up crookedly like the proverbial Cheshire cat.

It wasn't the answer Tom wanted, and his look of admiration turned to disdain.

Officer Harris, slow as molasses, it seemed, arrived at that moment.

"Handcuff him," Tom instructed.

But Seth would not give up without a fight. In a flash, he was off the floor and heading toward Mr. Delaney by the window, Officer Harris on his heels.

Haley thought Seth was after Will Delaney, who

apparently thought the same, since he made a dive behind the couch, but instead, Seth continued toward the fire escape.

"Stop!" Tom shouted, "Or I'll shoot."

Pausing, Seth stared at his wife. "I killed Joe Higgins. Delaney sent me to talk sense into him. Use my fists if I had to, he said. We fought because he was leaving the gang, refused the tattoo. It got out of hand and next thing I knew, I pulled out my blade." He sniffed. "We were friends. We fought together. I didn't mean for him to die. I didn't want any of them to die."

Seth Rosenbaum turned and jumped.

Samantha screamed, "Seth!"

Officer Bell, who couldn't get a fair shot out with Samantha in the way, now stood by her at the window. Samantha's hand was over her mouth, her eyes wide with horror.

"What is it?" Haley asked. Had Seth made it down the fire escape? Had he gotten away?

Tom Bell shook his head. "He jumped to the ground. He's dead."

25

*H*aley had barely registered the seriousness of Officer Bell's pronouncement, and even more astounding, Seth Rosenbaum's confession, when she caught sight of Will Delaney inching his way across the Persian carpet like a well-fed centipede.

She shouted, "Wait!"

But that only spurred Mr. Delaney to his feet and straight to the elevator door. Officer Harris ran after him, but his movements looked oddly stunted. Haley waited for him to pull out his pistol, but the elevator door opened before he could engage it, and Delaney slipped inside.

Officer Bell yelled, "Harris!" who jumped into action, belatedly, and disappeared into the elevator with Delaney.

Haley had a good idea who the mole was now and by the scowl on Officer Bell's face, she expected he had too. "Damn you, Harris!" Officer Bell shouted. He caught Haley's eye and said, "I'm taking the stairs!"

Samantha had crumpled to the floor, staring blankly ahead. Haley could only imagine all the conflicting emotions her friend felt and was uncertain what to do. Her instinct was to follow Officer Bell, but it would be heartless to leave Samantha.

Samantha seemed to read the uncertainty on Haley's face. With a faint nod of her head, she whispered, "Go."

"You're sure?"

"Yes," Strength of determination filled Samantha's eyes. "Go get him."

"Go," Mr. Milwaukee added. "I'll stay with her."

Haley gripped her gun and sprinted like she was running for home base in the ninth inning. Thanks to her athleticism, Haley soon caught up with Officer Bell. He acknowledged her with a look of surprise but kept running down the stairs.

They got to the lobby just as the elevator settled in from its descent.

Haley and Officer Bell held back around the corner, out of sight, and waited for Delaney and Harris to step out. Harris made a lame attempt at appearing as if he had Delaney by the arm, but when he glanced

LEE STRAUSS

around and assumed they were unwatched, he let go of his hold. They strolled out as if they were the best of friends without a care in the world.

Officer Bell called out, "Harris. Stop!"

Harris grabbed Delaney's arm, but Delaney wasn't having anything to do with that ruse and pushed Harris away. Harris, confirming Haley's suspicions that he was in cahoots with Delaney, bolted too. Haley—thankful she'd worn sensible utilitarian pumps on her feet—ran, she and Officer Bell on their heels.

Haley hadn't had time to digest that Samantha's husband had admitted to killing Joe, but Delaney was complicit, and she would not let him get away with murder.

Delaney and Harris raced toward the Union Boat Club, and Haley worried that they planned to escape by motorboat. If she and Officer Bell failed to apprehend them in time, they might get away.

Officer Bell heaved with heavy breaths, but Haley had to give him credit for keeping up—with his shorter, stockier physique, he didn't appear like a runner at first glance.

"Stop!" Officer Bell yelled, "Or I'll shoot."

And in a moment, Harris stopped.

Haley's heart skipped a beat. She and Officer Bell weren't the only ones with a gun. Harris raised his police weapon and fired.

Haley flinched, but she wasn't the target.

Officer Bell yelped and grabbed his arm.

Haley raised her weapon and aimed for Harris' legs. All that rabbit hunting she had done as a youth paid off. Harris crumpled to the ground.

Delaney, the only one without a gun, sprinted down the dock.

"Let him go," Officer Bell said, wincing through tight lips. "It's too dangerous."

The photographs of Joe, dead and dumped like garbage, flashed through Haley's mind. She couldn't let Delaney go. Her legs were already ahead of her heart, and she raced down the dock.

Will Delaney was many things, but a long-distance runner he was not. Haley suspected he hadn't had to exert himself physically for some time and found him bent over and panting as he tried to untie his polished wooden Chris Craft vessel from its mooring. Haley pulled back on the hammer of her Harrington & Richardson, which sounded with a satisfying *click*.

"It's over, Mr. Delaney," she said. "Put your hands up."

He straightened, ran a hand through his hair, and smirked. "What's this? A citizen's arrest?"

"Call it what you like. I'm not letting you get in that boat."

"If you kill me, you're no better than me."

"You're a monster, Mr. Delaney. I'm just a good shot."

In the distance, Haley heard police sirens. Probably someone from the Boat Club had called in the disturbance. She had only to bide her time.

Delaney had the same thought.

He saluted Haley then dove into the Charles River.

Haley couldn't believe his arrogance. Did he think he could swim across the river? Had he no idea about the currents?

Perhaps he thought it better to drown than to go to trial and hang.

Haley wasn't about to let justice not have its time in court. It was bad enough that Seth was dead.

She quickly untied the boat from the mooring. The keys, hanging from the ignition, made the rest easy. Haley had had experience driving boats when she'd stopped a rumrunner mid-crime.

As she suspected, Will Delaney struggled to stay afloat. Haley slowed the boat as she approached, brought it to a stop, then threw out the life preserver.

"I've heard drowning is a terrible way to die."

Putting the ladder out, she waited for Delaney to climb aboard. Keeping her gun aimed, she waited for him to catch his breath.

"You can drive us back," she said.

Drenched, his clothing clinging like an extra skin, he shivered. "And if I don't?"

"I'll be forced to shoot you. How much do you value your knees?"

26

---

*E*xcept for at the trial, and then only from across the room, Samantha hadn't seen Haley since the day Seth had jumped to his death.

Since the day Seth died, Samantha's losses had been significant: she'd lost her husband, her marriage, and the father of her child. Bina had been inconsolable, and Talia had grown sullen.

And she was sure she'd lost Haley as a friend. She'd called the morgue a couple of times, but Haley had either been immersed in something and unable to come to the telephone or out. Since Samantha didn't have a phone, Haley couldn't call her back, though she could've tried the paper, if she'd been determined.

Mr. August had let Samantha come back to work, and after a couple of awkward days with the guys in the pit, things returned to normal. She worked the ladies' pages, Fred hounded the athletes, Max chased Johnny around taking photographs, and Archie August bellowed for more stories.

Not everything returned to normal. Johnny hadn't sauntered over to her desk, hadn't flirted, or badgered her. He kept to himself, cigarette hanging out of his mouth, telephone to his ear.

Samantha supposed she could add him to her list of losses, though she wasn't sure what category to put him in.

Officer Bell remained a steady force—he called her once a day to make sure she was okay, reassured her that over time, people would forget Seth Rosenbaum, and that with Will Delaney out of the way, a new crime spree would replace them in short order. She'd apologized for doubting him and treating him poorly, but he waved her off, saying it was in the past.

Tom made her laugh, which was a difficult feat these days. Maybe, when this was all behind her, and her period of "mourning" was over, she'd take him up on that long-standing offer to go on a date.

Now, wearing a black day frock with a simple black lace collar, she stood at the door of the morgue. Her walk there had taken over an hour, and more than once, she'd almost talked herself into turning around.

But she was here now—she just had to knock and get it over with. Hopefully, enough time had passed that Haley could hear her apology and receive it.

ON THE OTHER side of the door, Haley focused on the paperwork due to be submitted or filed. She had just completed an autopsy—not murder related—and the family awaited the results. Her mind often betrayed her by revisiting the death of Seth Rosenbaum, and his last-minute confession. The trial had been difficult, especially the testimony that proved that Haley's brother Joe had been killed by Samantha's husband. Haley knew it wasn't fair of her, but she'd found it hard to face her friend after that.

Since then, Haley had gone through each day feeling numb. She'd spent much of her existence over the last seven years mulling over Joe's murder and brooding because the case had grown cold. Now that it'd been solved, she felt aimless. Joe's death had been such a driving factor in her life she felt lost without it, and this truth was shameful. Had her only reason for being been Joe's death?

She could hear Joe's voice in her head. *Don't be silly, Haley. Live a little.*

But how could she do that? Joe's unsolved murder

file had been a constant companion, a warped and morbid type of friend.

She felt alone and friendless.

There was Molly, but she was older, her housekeeper, more of a companion than a friend, and spent her free time with Dr. Guthrie. Dr. Mitchell, Gerald, was always there for her for comfort and support, but his wife was his priority and an invisible barrier.

Jack Thompson had clarified that he'd like to renew their relationship, short and fiery as it had been, but that was an invitation to romance. She wasn't ready to open her heart and mind.

Sam Hawke—Samantha Rosenbaum—had been a surprising but unlikely friendship. Haley, wealthy, single, and educated, wouldn't normally find friendship with someone who eked out a living to support a family, and a reporter at that.

But Samantha's husband had murdered Joe.

Even though Haley knew it wasn't Samantha's doing, she found it hard to separate the two things. It was unfair. Not just to Samantha, but to Haley.

She missed her friend.

When Haley heard someone knocking, images of Samantha over the last few months doing the same thing flashed across her mind. She headed for the door. Wouldn't it be something if it were—

"Samantha?"

"Hello, Haley. I hope you don't mind."

Haley blinked at Samantha dressed in black, not used to the somber look, but right for new widowhood. "No, of course not. Come in. I was just thinking of you."

"Molly said you were working late."

Haley had been doing that a lot lately. It was the best way to keep her mind from wandering places she didn't want it to go.

"Come in."

Samantha reached into her oversized handbag. "I brought this." She pulled out a bottle of Canadian whiskey. "Compliments of Mr. Delaney, actually. Turns out, in some regards, he was a man of his word."

William Delaney had been convicted on several counts of murder, running illegal gambling rings in street fighting, and money laundering. The date of his hanging was yet to be determined, but Haley found, in some small way, that she'd avenged her brother's death by capturing the man who'd enticed him into the fight club and had sent Seth Rosenbaum after him.

Testimony against Seth Rosenbaum hadn't shed a good light on the man's life. He accidentally killed Joe —now Father O'Hara's story about Jesus and Judas made sense. It's about betrayal. It was about betrayal.

After that unfortunate event, Delaney had forced

Seth into working as his hatchet man. It was either that or death whether at Delaney's hand or by the noose. Perhaps that was why Seth had fled the city—he didn't want to be Delaney's assassin.

Once Delaney had discovered Seth had returned to Boston, he put the man back to work. A threat against Seth's family, against Samantha and Talia, had made him comply. First, Cormac Keating for challenging Delaney's leadership—the note Samantha had found in his pocket had been a warning from Seth—then Mulryan who couldn't pay his debts, and finally, the John Doe, a misfit fighter who apparently had a big mouth Delaney wanted silenced.

Haley glanced at Samantha with sympathy. It couldn't be easy to discover your husband was a repeat murderer.

Haley produced two glasses and Samantha poured. Raising their glasses, they toasted.

"Cheers," Samantha said.

"Cheers," Haley echoed.

After a moment, Samantha said, "I'm sorry."

"I'm the one who should apologize," Haley said. "You didn't kill Joe. I'm sorry for taking it out on you."

They shared silence as forgiveness was accepted.

"I came to Seth's funeral." Haley felt she should make the disclosure. She'd hidden herself in the sea of black at the back of the small crowd, not wanting to be noticed. She wasn't sure why she'd gone. Maybe just to see it for herself. A sense of closure. It had broken her heart to see Mrs. Rosenbaum, so frail and petite, curled up in her grief. Little Talia had worn an appropriate pout, more likely overwhelmed by the intensity of the funeral and her grandmother's wailing than by sadness over a man she hadn't really known. Samantha had been dry-eyed and stoic, keeping the small family together.

"I know," Samantha replied, to Haley's surprise. "You're rather tall, even when you slouch."

"Oh."

"They've set a date for Delaney's hanging."

"They have?"

"Yes. The telegraph came to the paper this afternoon."

"You're back at work, then?"

"I am. It's good. I've discovered I like my job, and I'm glad to be back. Bina needs something to do, more than ever now, and Talia is a great comfort to her."

"I'm glad to hear it."

"I'm lying low," Samantha motioned at her black dress, "but I just can't sit around."

"It's quite understandable," Haley said. Work had been her lifeline after Joe had died.

"Now that I'm back at the paper," Samantha

began, "we might run into each other again. On the job."

"Or off," Haley offered.

Samantha tipped her glass of whiskey. "Or off."

Haley clinked her glass against her friend's. "I look forward to it."

27

FOUR MONTHS LATER

*T*he last days of 1931 saw the end of many things that had become normal in Haley's life. Her brother Benjamin, who worked their family farm along with his wife, Lorene, came into town with their adopted baby boy in tow, and even their wayward brother Harley-James traveled to Boston all the way from California, so they could celebrate and honor Joseph's life.

It was a bittersweet gathering, and the first time Haley had shed tears since first learning about Joe's death. With the case solved and behind her, Haley knew it was time to let that burden go. Joe wouldn't want her to continue the way she had, his death consuming her life.

This wasn't the only event to take place in October. Dr. Guthrie announced his retirement and had fought hard for the mayor to give Haley his position. That she was female had proven to be a high liability, but in the end, Dr. Guthrie had shown how Haley's work should be judged on its own merits regardless of her gender. It was a great victory for feminism everywhere when she'd been granted the title of Chief Medical Examiner.

But her gain at work was a loss at home. When Dr. Guthrie retired, he'd also proposed to Molly. They had a December wedding, and Molly moved in with her new husband right after their honeymoon in England and Ireland. She'd sent Haley a postcard filled with exclamation marks on how much she was enjoying an English Christmas on the arm of her new husband. Haley had enjoyed the solitude of her apartment for a while but now admitted to feeling rather lonely, especially coming home to an empty house. Particularly since Molly had taken Mr. Midnight with her.

Besides Seth Rosenbaum, the fall had claimed two more lives in Haley's circle. The first was Gerald Mitchell's wife. She'd developed a cancerous tumor that had taken her quickly. Gerald was bereft, but had confessed to Haley he felt guilty for the sense of relief that had come with her passing.

Another loss was Jack Thompson. Haley had been wise to keep an emotional distance. He'd proven once again to be a slave to his restless streak, and had announced suddenly, on a cold day in November, he was going to Peru.

Adios.

Not all was terrible, though. Out of loss, there is sometimes a newness of life, a new lease of sorts, a new perspective. Haley, having always put Gerald firmly in the category of friendship—propriety had demanded it —had found she'd formed feelings on a deeper level. It would never be the sizzle and spice she'd felt with Jack, but it was safe and secure. Gentle and kind. And Gerald made her laugh, not an easy feat these days, and something Jack could never do.

When the new year had dawned, Haley got new roommates.

Because of the second death.

After her son died, Bina Rosenbaum had seemed to lose the will to live. *She was old and tired*, Haley thought, *and sad with the weight of her hard life. Even little Talia could no longer ignite her joy.*

She'd succumbed to pneumonia during a cold, blizzard night. The snow had fallen thickly and wet, making it hard for it to be removed and vehicles to travel, especially down clogged, narrow lanes like Stillman Street. Haley had practically had to hike a mountain of snow to get to the front door of the tenements. Mrs. Rosenbaum was dead by then. Haley had been called in as the medical examiner.

Haley awoke to the sounds of low voices coming from the kitchen. She smiled at the image of Samantha and Talia eating breakfast and rose with a skip to her step that she didn't quite understand. She'd often avoid the meal altogether, but now, she found she looked forward to the morning meal and this new tradition.

"Good morning," she said as she entered the kitchen.

Samantha and Talia sang in unison, "Good morning."

Haley took her place at the table, where eggs and bacon along with toast and jam, awaited. "Smells terrific."

Samantha poured Haley a cup of coffee, "You say that every morning."

Haley added cream and sugar and gave her brew a good stir. "It's true every morning."

Talia giggled. "You're funny, Auntie Haley."

Haley smiled. "Thank you." The attachment that had grown between her and the young girl surprised her. She imagined this would be as close as she'd get to experiencing what it might be like to have a daughter.

"Are you excited about school today?" Haley said.

Talia nodded, her blond curls bouncing.

"You are?" Haley said, her astonishment not wholly exaggerated. Talia usually wrinkled her nose and pouted at the question. Haley had convinced

Samantha to allow her to pay for private school, one with a good science program.

"We're going to the museum today," Talia said. "I'm going to see dinosaur bones!"

Samantha laughed, and Haley joined in. Once, Haley had worried that Samantha might never smile again.

With the new year came new hope.

After breakfast, the morning hustle began with all three getting ready to be gone for the day. Samantha and Talia caught the bus, while Haley drove her DeSoto to the hospital. In the morgue, Haley settled into her new office and enjoyed the view through the windows of the other desks and operating lounge.

Haley had offered Mr. Martin her old position as assistant Chief Medical Examiner and watched him busy with paperwork at her old desk.

She reviewed the work that had come through the morgue over the holidays, making sure the autopsy reports were completed and bodies released on time. The telephone in her office rang—a new addition to the morgue—and she answered it.

"Hello, Gerald," she said, feeling the smile tug upwards. She could imagine him on the other side of the line, with kind eyes, his salt-and-pepper hair oiled back, and his white doctor's coat crisp. He wanted to know if she'd like to see the latest Clara Bow movie that evening.

"Yes," she said. "I'd love to."

SAMANTHA STILL WORE BLACK, but now she added hints of color to her wardrobe, lavender mostly. A ribbon on her hat, a sash at the waist. Sometimes, like today, a tri-strand of artificial pearls against her throat. As soon as the snow melted, she decided, she'd put the mourning dresses away for good.

Haley's invitation for her and Talia to move in had been a shock. After so many losses, her offer had been a beacon of light too generous for Samantha to accept. But Haley had been convincing. How could Samantha raise a daughter on her own, in a tenement building that harbored black mold among other human types of dangers?

"You're a single woman with a child. It's not safe."

Haley had had a good point. There were more than a few unsavory types. A man deprived of work and food wasn't often the best company for people like Samantha and Talia. They made a bargain: Samantha would do light cooking and housework to help fill the hole that Molly had left, in exchange for rent. Mr. August had agreed to give her fewer hours so she could perform those domestic duties and pick up her daughter from school. If work became demanding, Mrs. Berrymaple next door offered to watch Talia.

Lemonade out of lemons.

Life was different with Bina and Seth gone, and sadly, Samantha had to admit, a lot better. Seth had left a surprise behind. Samantha had found a key among his things that fit a locker at the train station. Inside she'd found a duffle bag containing several thousand dollars.

Samantha hadn't known what to do with the money. She'd had to assume it had possibly been obtained by Seth through nefarious means, but how did she know that for sure? Seth had never told her what he'd been doing for the last seven years. Maybe he'd been working somewhere and had saved it for when he came home.

There was a slight chance that the version of events could be true.

Regardless, there was no way to track the money. Haley had convinced her to keep it for Talia's sake. She'd inquired discreetly of Detective Cluney if he'd heard of a moderate sum of money going missing anywhere in the United States. There was nothing to link Seth to a significant crime, like a bank or train robbery. Haley suggested Samantha put the money in trust for Talia's future.

Now that Samantha was an official widow, she was

free to date again. Tom Bell had been waiting for this moment, and just as Samantha was about to agree on a date, he'd got engaged to another lady!

Good for him. Miss Hyde seemed like a nice gal, and Tom deserved to be happy.

The pit was busy with fingers flying on typewriters, conversations on telephones, and the telegraph noisily spitting out papers. Samantha worked on an article for the ladies' column, "A Modern Woman's New Year's Resolutions". She hadn't been on a big investigation since *she*'d been the big case. Will Delaney's arrest and subsequent hanging overshadowed Seth's involvement, but it didn't keep her, as his widow, out of the limelight. She'd been hounded by the press at competing papers for weeks, and now had a new sensitivity for people when she was after a story.

Of course, she'd given the *Boston Daily Record* an exclusive. Mr. August rewarded her with a nice raise too.

Samantha watched Johnny Milwaukee out of the corner of her eye—a bad habit she'd developed lately. He hunched over his typewriter, a cigarette balanced at the corner of his mouth, his eyes intense as he plucked away at the keys, one finger at a time. He glanced up and caught her looking. She quickly stared back at the roll of paper in her typewriter, unable to focus.

She sensed, rather than saw, him approach her desk.

"Hey doll, whatcha workin' on?"

She forced a look of disinterest as she leaned back in her chair. "Not much. Gotta New Year's goal you wanna share with the ladies?"

He leaned against her desk and rubbed his clean-shaven chin in thought. "I think a gal should consider love in the new year. Fresh leaf, fresh start. That kind of thing."

Samantha stared back coyly. "Good idea, Mr. Milwaukee. Got anything more specific than that?"

He grinned and leaned in. "How about lunch? They make a great bisque soup around the corner."

"Hmm," Samantha said. She was teasing Johnny, but the red growing in her cheeks was sure to give her away. "I dunno. I might be busy."

"I've got a new lead."

Samantha sat up. "You do?"

He winked. "Is that a yes, Miss Hawke."

Samantha grabbed her hat. "It's a yes."

To MAKE sure you don't miss the next new release, be sure to sign up for Lee's readers' list and get 4 FREE short stories!

https://www.leestraussbooks.com/subscribe-four-free/

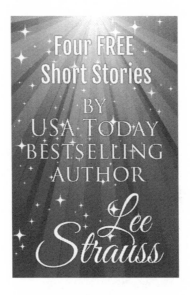

Don't miss the next Ginger Gold Mystery NEW RELEASE!

MURDER ON FLEET STREET

Murder's a Deadly Secret

MRS. GINGER REED—THE former Lady Gold— thought her past was dead and buried, but when the mysterious death of a British Secret Service agent threatens to expose her own Great War secrets, she's faced with an unimaginable dilemma: break her legal vow to the Official Secrets Act or join the agency again, something she's loathed to do.

Because once they own your soul, there's no getting it back.

READ ON FOR AN EXERPT

Coming January 2020. This book will not be available for preorder so be sure to follow Lee on social media or join her readers' list to stay informed.

https://www.leestraussbooks.com/subscribe-four-free/

Learn more at leestraussbooks.com

While you're waiting for this new release why not try
MURDER AT EATON SQUARE.

Murder's Bad Karma. . .

. . .

LIFE COULDN'T BE BETTER on Eaton Square Gardens where the most prestigious families lived, until one of their own dies and it's *murder*.

Ginger and Basil are on the case, but it's not a simple glass of bubbly fizz. The more the clues present themselves, the trickier the puzzle gets, and Ginger feels she's on a wild goose chase.

But as someone close to the victim so aptly quips, "One shouldn't commit murder. It's bad karma."

Reaping what one sows is hardly a great cup of tea.

ABOUT THE AUTHOR

Lee Strauss is a USA TODAY bestselling author of The Ginger Gold Mysteries series, The Higgins & Hawke Mystery series (cozy historical mysteries), A Nursery Rhyme Mystery series (mystery suspense), The Perception series (young adult dystopian), The Light & Love series (sweet romance), The Clockwise Collection (YA time travel romance), and young adult historical fiction with over a million books read. She has titles published in German, Spanish and Korean, and a growing audio library.

When Lee's not writing or reading she likes to cycle, hike, and play pickleball. She loves to drink caffè lattes and red wines in exotic places, and eat dark chocolate anywhere.

For more info on books by Lee Strauss and her social media links, visit leestraussbooks.com. To make sure you don't miss the next new release, be sure to sign up for her readers' list and get 4 FREE short stories!

https://www.leestraussbooks.com/subscribe-four-free/

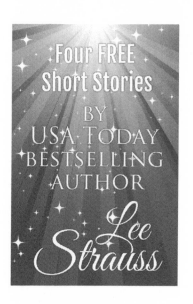

fun discussions ○ special giveaways ○ exclusive content

Join my Facebook readers group for fun discussions and first-to-know exclusives!

Did you know you can follow your favorite authors on Bookbub? If you subscribe to Bookbub — (and if you don't, why don't you? - They'll send you daily emails alerting you to sales and new releases on just the kind of books you like to read!) — follow me to make sure you don't miss the next Ginger Gold Mystery!

www.leestraussbooks.com
leestraussbooks@gmail.com

companion short stories)

HIGGINS & HAWKE MYSTERY SERIES (cozy 1930s historical)

The 1930s meets Rizzoli & Isles in this friendship depression era cozy mystery series.

A NURSERY RHYME MYSTERY SERIES(mystery/sci fi)

Marlow finds himself teamed up with intelligent and savvy Sage Farrell, a girl so far out of his league he feels blinded in her presence - literally - damned glasses! Together they work to find the identity of @gingerbreadman. Can they stop the killer before he strikes again?

THE PERCEPTION TRILOGY (YA dystopian mystery)

Zoe Vanderveen is a GAP—a genetically altered person. She lives in the security of a walled city on prime water-front property along side other equally beautiful people with extended life spans. Her brother Liam is missing. Noah Brody, a boy on the outside, is the only one who can help ~ but can she trust him?

Perception

Volition

Contrition

LIGHT & LOVE (sweet romance)

Set in the dazzling charm of Europe, follow Katja, Gabriella, Eva, Anna and Belle as they find strength, hope and love.

Sing me a Love Song

Your Love is Sweet

In Light of Us

Lying in Starlight

PLAYING WITH MATCHES (WW2 history/romance)

A sobering but hopeful journey about how one young Germany boy copes with the war and propaganda. Based on true events.

As Elle Lee Strauss

THE CLOCKWISE COLLECTION (YA time travel romance)

Casey Donovan has issues: hair, height and uncontrollable trips to the 19th century! And now this ~ she's accidentally taken Nate Mackenzie, the cutest boy in the school, back in time. Awkward.

Clockwise

Clockwiser

Like Clockwork

Counter Clockwise

Clockwork Crazy

Standalones

Seaweed

Love, Tink

MURDER ON FLEET STREET

Chapter 1

Mrs. Ginger Reed, also known around the city of London as Lady Gold, loved a good party. And if the official adoption of her son, Scout, wasn't a fabulous reason to celebrate, then she couldn't think of what was.

A three-piece band had set up in the corner of the drawing room at Hartigan House, Ginger's childhood home in South Kensington, and begun to play.

"Basil, love," she said, clasping her husband's arm, "we simply must dance."

He smiled back at her, his hazel eyes twinkling in a manner that made Ginger's heart burst with pride. She'd chosen her rose georgette gown with the sequinned double-scalloped skirt especially because she knew it was one of his favourites. Her long strand of beads complemented the pearly-white bead trim in the hem, and a dramatic red bow was stitched low on the hipline. She'd pinned back her red bob, newly styled in finger waves that morning, with a delicate hair clip, trimmed with rhinestones.

Dancing was a favourite pastime for Ginger and Basil. They'd met properly for the first time on the dance floor of a club on the SS *Rosa*, on a steamship journey from Boston to Liverpool. It was also where they'd both met their son, Scout, who'd worked in the belly of the ship tending the animals including in the pet kennel where Ginger's Boston terrier Boss had spent time.

"Isn't it funny how things turn out?" she said as Basil swept her around the drawing room, swirling past large portraits on ivory and green art deco wallpaper. It wasn't as large as the ball room found in some houses, but, with the furniture pushed back, it was plenty big enough for a crowd this size. Felicia, Ginger's youthful former sister-in-law who also lived at Hartigan House, was dancing with a rather attractive constable who worked under Basil in his position of a chief inspector at Scotland Yard. Mr. Fulton, Scout's tutor, stood on the sidelines watching wistfully. Felicia, catching the young teacher's eye, raised a thinly plucked, deeply arched eyebrow and winked, causing the poor man to blush.

Ginger clucked her tongue. What was she to do with Felicia and her "Bright Young Thing" ways?

Ambrosia, known publicly as the Dowager Lady Gold, the matriarch in the house, sat upright in one of the green velvet wingback chairs, her grey hair tucked under a feather-rich hat, and bejewelled fingers clasping her walking stick. Her wrinkled face was stony, showing neither delight nor distaste, but Ginger knew her former grandmother struggled with Ginger's decision to adopt what she called a "street urchin".

However, Hartigan House was her home and Ambrosia, a long-term guest, was wise enough, after making her original objections known, to keep her thoughts on the matter to herself.

The boy in question played with Boss in the corner by the fireplace. He'd put on weight since joining her family and, though small for his age, had grown at least four inches. Some had wondered aloud, and not so sensitively at that, why Ginger, if she must adopt, hadn't chosen an infant? Surely there were plenty of babies around, and from better stock?

She couldn't explain how fate had stepped in. When a heart loves, it simply loves unconditionally.

When the music ended, Ginger approached the drinks trolley which was manned by Clement, her man of many talents. Primarily her gardener, he also took care of the horses, the cars, and stepped in as a footman when required.

He handed her a glass of champagne.

"Thank you, Clement," she said, and glancing back at Basil, added, "Darling?"

Basil stepped in behind her. "I'll have a gin and tonic, Clement, if you would."

"Certainly, sir."

Basil touched Ginger's elbow, then left to join a group of men who'd congregated together and were immersed in what appeared to be a rousing conversation about the stock market.

"Capital, my good fellow," one said.

And another, "I'm making a fortune hardly lifting a finger."

Pushing back an underlying sense of fatigue, Ginger joined Ambrosia who was having a hard time not looking bored by their neighbour Mrs. Schofield who sat in the next chair.

"How serendipitous that the Adoption Act should come into affect just when your granddaughter decided to take in the stable boy."

Ambrosia's feathers were ruffled.

"He was Ginger's *ward*. Not a stable boy."

Mrs. Schofield, her white hair knotted on the top of her head in a Victorian-style bun, had a sparkle of mischief in her eye, and Ginger was quite certain the elderly lady enjoyed tormenting her friend.

"And now he's your grandson!"

Ambrosia's wide blue eyes slid to Mrs. Schofield. "You know full well that Ginger was married to my grandson. Now that he's gone and she's remarried, we're not actually related."

"Not by blood, but surely by circumstance?"

Ginger felt a twinge of pity for the dowager. "Champagne, Grandmother? I've not touched it yet."

"Yes, please." She held out a leathery hand. "Will you join us?" Then, lowering her voice, yet well aware that Mrs. Schofield could hear, "before she talks my ear off."

Ginger bit her lip to hold in a smile and took an empty seat.

"Alfred sends his regrets," Mrs. Schofield said, "but asked me to offer his congratulations." Alfred was Mrs. Schofield's grandson and a person of questionable character. Ginger had felt an uncharitable sense of relief when he'd declined the invitation.

"That's quite all right," she replied. "I understand that he's a busy man."

Lord and Lady Whitmore, neighbours on Mallowan Court as well, were amongst the many guests. Lord Whitmore, a distinguished-looking gentleman in his late fifties, and Ginger shared a confidence—they were both involved with the British secret service, though Ginger had stepped out after the war. It was a fact they both pretended to know nothing about, and anyone in the room would likely be shocked if they knew the truth, including all the members of Ginger's own family.

Lord Whitmore splintered away from his wife, pulled into the grouping of men by the lure of money talk. Lady Whitmore, in her constant effort to hold on to her youth, wore a fashionable turban over short hair. She caught Ginger's eye and with the lampshade fringe of her gown brushing her calves, eased over to join the ladies.

"Such a lovely party," Lady Whitmore said. "The last party I attended was Lady Roth's birthday party. Were you there? No? Yes, well, don't feel bad about not being invited. The occasion fell flat in the end. There certainly weren't any newspaper men present."

Ginger followed the direction of Lady Whitmore's gaze and grinned at the sight of Mr. Blake Brown from the *Daily News*. Wearing a tweed suit over a slight stomach bulge, the wear-line of a hat now removed over thinning hair, and a camera bag strapped over his shoulder, he was rather hard to miss. Ginger had called the *Daily News* hoping to get a bit of coverage in the social pages. It was a stopgap effort on her part to stop tongues from wagging and to answer once and for all the probable awkward questions that were sure to arise. Though her adoption of Scout Elliot wasn't exactly scandalous, it was most certainly unorthodox and fodder for eager gossipers.

This was probably why Lord and Lady Whitmore had accepted Ginger's invitation. The Whitmores weren't close friends, but living in the immediate vicinity had merited consideration, and Lady Whitmore wasn't one to miss out social highlights. This party would give her something to jaw about to her friends for weeks.

Ginger excused herself and greeted the journalist.

"Thank you for coming, Mr. Brown. I know it's not your usual type of story."

She and Mr. Brown were acquainted, and though their relationship had started out on a rocky footing, Ginger now trusted him, as far as one could trust a reporter.

"Your parties aren't usually normal parties, Mrs. Reed."

Ginger fiddled with the long beads around her neck. The last two events Ginger had hosted, and which Mr. Brown had covered, had involved a dead body. She sincerely hoped that wouldn't be the case tonight.

"I can assure you that I'm doing my best to make sure that everyone leaves here alive."

Ginger, her T-strap shoes tapping along the wooden floors, gracefully made her way to the grand piano in the corner. After motioning to the band to end their set, she tickled the ivory keys. The room, subconsciously aware of the change, quieted.

"Now that I have your attention," Ginger began. She stood, catching Basil and Scout's gazes and nodded subtly for them to join her. "I'd like to make a toast. Please everyone, get your drinks."

Pippins, Ginger's butler, took the cue and brought over two flutes of champagne and a glass of cola for Scout.

"Thank you, Pips," Ginger said. Of all the people in the room, Ginger had known Clive Pippins the longest and considered the spry blue-eyed septuagenarian, to be more like family than a mere employee.

Once everyone had a drink and was facing Ginger, she began, "Thank you, everyone, for joining us as we celebrate the official adoption of our son, Scout." Ginger placed a hand on Scout's thin shoulder, feeling a twinge of sympathy as he blushed with embarrassment at all the attention. Scout *had* grown up on the streets of London, and survival almost always meant remaining invisible and out of sight of the average citizen, ostensibly because it was easier to rob them that way. This party was Ginger and Basil's attempt to get the facts out before the tabloids could run amok with half-truths and falsehoods.

"We are pleased that the British government has begun to legislate in the matter of adoption, for the sake of both the parents and the children. Scout will from here on in be legally known as Mr. Samuel Reed, and affectionately as Scout."

Scout was in fact the boy's given name, christened as such by his natural mother. However, there were no actual documents reporting his birth. Ginger only knew of Scout's birthday because his cousin, Marvin, currently engaged with the Royal Navy, remembered the date. Samuel was a name she, Scout, and Basil had decided upon together.

Mr. Brown slouched about as he snapped photographs, as if hunching low would disguise him somehow, or minimize the pop of the flash pan, or diminish the smoke left in his wake.

Though most of the people in the room were dear friends or family, or at least comfortable acquaintances, there was a notable absence. Basil's parents strongly opposed their son and daughter-in-law's decision to adopt Scout, finding him a threat to the "bloodline" and distribution of family wealth, and had threatened to withhold Basil's inheritance. When they'd learned that their son would defy them, they decided they needed to go on a trip to recover and work out what it would mean for their future. The last Ginger heard, they were on a ship headed to South Africa.

Ginger, who'd been unable to conceive, either with her first husband Daniel, Lord Gold, or with Basil, was just thankful to God that he'd brought Scout into their lives, and that she was now a mother, and they, a family of three. She couldn't have been happier.

Basil lifted his glass. "Please join me as we celebrate our good fortune."

A chorus of "hear, hear," resounded as glasses clinked and then were sipped from.

Scout tugged on Ginger's arm.

"Can me and Boss go to my room now? It's awful stuffy in here."

Boss, at Scout's feet, wagged his stubby tail and panted with his big doggy smile as if he couldn't agree with Scout's sentiment more.

"It's 'May Boss and I' and yes, you may."

Ginger grinned as she watched the boy and dog dodge adult bodies and disappear out of the double doors that opened to the entrance and grand staircase to the next floor. She gave her empty glass to her maid Lizzie, a petite young lady, who cleaned up after the guests with experienced proficiency, then nodded to the band to strike up a again.

"Make it a quick one," she said.

The introductory notes of "Five Foot Two, Eyes of Blue" were played and Ginger grabbed Basil's hand.

"I love a good Charleston," she said as her heels snapped backward to the beat. Basil held her in his arms and matched her move for move. Ginger laughed heartily. Happiness like this mustn't be taken for granted. One never knew what the next day would bring.

Get it on Amazon

ACKNOWLEDGMENTS

Some things are worth repeating:

Thank you to these wonderful people who make the magic happen.

Angelika Offenwanger - developmental editor, who reads the first dreadful drafts and helps me keep the story from falling off the rails. She's also a friend. (Thanks for your support!)

Robbie Bryant - line editor, who cleans up the first "finished" draft.

Heather Belleguelle - beta reader extraordinaire, who helps me to polish the story and complete the wordsmithing. (The day you quit is the day I quit. 😄)

Shadi Bleiken - administrator and social media guru, who helps me keep all the strings tied together and get the word out. She's a gift to La Plume Press and to the Strauss family!

Norm Strauss - partner in life and in crime. I love how we can work and play together and never stop finding something to laugh about.

Made in the USA
Middletown, DE
11 December 2020

27293680R00151